The Doctor's Curse

The Doctor's Curse

Heather Quinto

TruRealm Media
www.trurealmmedia.com

The Doctor's Curse

This book is a work of fiction. Any references to historical events, real people, or real places are used fictitiously. Any resemblance to actual events, places, or persons, living or dead, is entirely coincidental.
The text of this book is initially set in Saratoga Springs, NY

This book is the continuation of "The Doctor's Estate" published in 2019.

ISBN: 978-0-578-91444-2

Published by TruRealm Media

trurealmmedia.com

Clovis, CA

Author's Note

With sequels, it can be nerve-wracking because people usually seem to enjoy the original better. With the second installment of this series, I was excited and honored to be able to bring Ted alive again. With any book, I strive to be as unique as possible. I like to call myself a 'genre bender' because I tend to combine more than one genre to create a truly original novel, which is exactly what I did here. This won't be your typical horror novel because it's not meant to be. This is an adventure into the life of Ted, which doesn't fit into a neat little box. I do hope you enjoy this ride and learn something new along the way.

-Heather Marie Quinto

Acknowledgments

I'd like to thank my roommates Jasmine, Emily, Shayne, and Sam for the support and help with inspiration. I'd also like to thank my partner, Josh, for being supportive of my career and always being there for me.

About The Author

Heather Quinto is a Yaqui Native American, and she resides in Fresno, California with her life partner and many animals. She has a BA in Creative Writing/English with a minor in Marketing from Southern New Hampshire University. She is the author of the paranormal/fantasy novel, *Inhuman,* and a spiritual/romance short story titled *In Love and Death*. She helped write *The Doctor's Estate* and *The Doctor's Curse* with Jesus Martinez, who is the creator of the story.

Heather always had a strong urge to write and create imaginative stories ever since she could pick up a pencil. She started off by drawing picture books when she was four, and began writing short stories when she was eight years old. Heather's main inspiration behind writing is to be able to leave the greatest impact on whomever picks up one of her books by challenging her readers to think differently. As a writer, Heather strives to add hidden themes within her books and layers of symbolism in the plot and characters to add a more flavorful storytelling. You can read and reread one of her novels and find a whole new perspective of the story each time.

"Writing is a powerful tool. All I need is a pen and paper, and I can change the world." -Heather Quinto

Chapter One

Ted's New Awakening

I stared straight ahead at the wooden hand rest of the chair in my doctor's office. Focusing on my breaths, I tried to steady my anxious thoughts. I rubbed my eyes, fighting sleep.

"Are the nightmares still happening?" asked the doctor in front of me.

I fidgeted in my seat. "Yeah."

"What was it this time?"

Running my fingers through my hair, I let out a slow breath. "It's the same as always. I'm in the house in the basement, and something happens."

"How are you feeling now that we bring up the house?"

My eyes snapped up from the chair to my doctor who sat cross-legged in front of me. I continued with clenching my jaw. His wispy hair stood up on end from running his fingers through it. His thick-rimmed glasses made his eyes bigger through the lenses. I shrugged at his question. "I'd rather just forget about it," I said.

"That does not tell me how you feel."

1

Letting out an agitated sigh, I peered out the window before eyeing the digital clock, which sat on the desk below it. I had ten more minutes of this crap. Ten more minutes and I was free.

"Can I take a guess at how you may be feeling?"

"Fine," I breathed.

"You're nervous. I can tell by the way you immediately started shaking your knee when I mentioned the house."

Peering down at my leg, I stopped. I hadn't noticed.

"Your jaw muscles are tightening, which tells me either agitation or nervousness. Perhaps both. You are refusing to meet my eyes and you keep staring at the clock, which tells me you don't want to be here."

The only reason I was here talking to Dr. Whitaker was because my sister and Christina insisted on it after the incident with my father.

Dr. Whitaker took off his glasses and sighed. "We won't make any progress if you refuse to engage with me."

"But I'm fine," I said, more to convince myself than him.

Whitaker licked his lips and nodded. He sat up in his chair and said, "I think you should see a psychiatrist. You display symptoms of anxiety, depression, and you have PTSD from that house."

I shook my head, refusing to accept this man's words. How could he tell all that from my just sitting here?

His tone implored me. "Something significant happened there, and it's okay to need some healing from that."

My phone's alarm went off, which meant it was time for me to go. I set it because I wanted to spend as little time here as possible. I managed a short smile. "Okay. Thanks for your time." Quickly grabbing my jacket, I headed out the door. I couldn't wait to get home so I could workout and get ready for work. All I needed was more time to grieve my mother's death and get over what happened at the house. I didn't need meds for that.

Sitting in my small truck, I sighed before resting my head on the steering wheel. It had been a couple of years since my mother's death and three years since I left the damn house. Still, my mother's death wasn't getting any easier. I willed myself to sit back up and started the engine. The crisp morning air turned my breath to fog as I willed myself to sit up and start the engine. Still cold, I rubbed my hands together before cranking the head and then the radio.

My favorite radio station's DJ spoke, *So in other news, they are reportedly demolishing the infamous Saratoga Springs mansion.*

My heart constricted, and I swallowed to try and rid myself of the tightness which formed in my chest.

Finally, they are getting rid of that eyesore. The house has a long history of being haunted and became even more famous after the hostage situation that took place there only three years ago.

I turned off the radio. There was no way I could bring myself to listen to the broadcast anymore. Then again, I couldn't bring myself to get over my mother's passing either.

Each time I thought of her, it was like a tiny needle poked at my heart, leaving a burning sensation in its wake. Seeing the mansion, which I had intended to renovate for

3

her, in line to be demolished was like the final nail in the coffin. It cemented her being gone from this world for good. It was unreasonable to think of the mansion like that, but a part of me was attached to the property along with part of my mother's memory. The house being destroyed also destroyed a part of her and me.

That's in the past, Ted. Let it go. The house doesn't matter. You have moved on, remember?

I shifted to drive and made my way back to my apartment. It was a small and quant place in a good part of town. The building was relatively old, and the walls were thin, so you could hear what was going on with the neighbors from time to time. It was a two-story brick building that sat right at the corner, making the building curve at the front. Parking across the street, I walked over to the entrance. My apartment was located on the upper level, and the metal staircase shook a bit underneath my weight. They needed to replace the damn steps. The smell of aged mildew infiltrated my nostrils. They also needed to add air fresheners.

Once inside my apartment, I looked over my shoulder at Christina, who was sipping on her coffee as she stuffed her wallet and phone into her purse. "Hey, you're back already," she said. "Just in time to see me off to work." She looked up at me and smiled. "How was it today?" Her hair was extra curly this morning, and it complemented her face well as it cascaded down her shoulders. Her bright eyes peered up at me in that loving way that made me feel like everything was going to be okay. She was downright beautiful.

Shrugging off my jacket, I hung it on the hook attached to the door. I placed my keys into our designated basket that sat on a small table by the entrance. "Same as always."

Christina let out a breath through her nose which told me she was a bit frustrated. "Ya never gonna get anywhere if ya don't open up to the doctor." She took out her Chapstick and applied it to her lips. "I'm on medication for my chronic anxiety, and there ain't no shame in it, hon."

Walking over to the coffee pot, I poured myself a drink. "I'm not that bad off." Meds were for people who were sick. Not for people like me that'd had a bad experience. I just had to shake it off.

Christina got up. "Try one of my meds and see how it makes ya feel." She made her way over to me and kissed me on the cheek. "Nothing permanent, but just see if ya feel better. Have a great day, hon. I'll bring home something nice for dinner."

I couldn't help but smile as I looked down at her. "You have a good day too."

She made her way to the door, putting on her purple beanie and scarf, which complemented her light-brown skin well. She blew me a kiss and winked before shutting the door behind her.

I sat at the kitchen table, sipping my coffee. Peering down, I saw my pocket-sized notepad, which I used it to help keep track of how I was healing. Christina insisted on me doing that every night before bed. She refused to turn off the lights unless I filled it in. She was determined to help me, even if I didn't want her to. Moving in with her had made me learn a few things about her. One, she was a neat freak like

5

me. Two, she loved to craft whenever she was nervous. And three, she was always nervous, which made her want to have control over things.

I picked up the notepad and flipped through the past several weeks. Each day started the same, and each day ended with irritability. Not wanting to take it out on Christina, I'd often say I was tired and pretend to go to bed. So far, I had done an excellent job of keeping myself from lashing out at her. I couldn't say the same for my friends.

After I finished my coffee, I grabbed my workout towel and headed downstairs to the workout room of the apartment complex. I had to sell all my gym equipment because I wouldn't have space in the apartment, plus it was pointless since the complex had its tiny gym. It wasn't much, but it worked. Selling the house made me a little wealthier than before, and it enabled me to be able to pay off the mortgage. In the end, I had twenty thousand left over. The legend of what happened there with me made the home a haunted attraction. The new owner tried to salvage the house by making it into a historical monument since it had a long history, but that plan fell under. It was a bed and breakfast for a short bit, but the owner couldn't keep up with it, and now it sat abandoned, waiting for its next victim.

Stop thinking about the house. I stepped into the workout room. The air was moist from its last visitor, which the foam mats soaked up and made the room feel damp. Setting my towel down on the side of the power rack, I put the weight plates on the sides of the bar. Working out was a sure-fire way to put my mind at ease. It was my therapy. My knuckles whitened as I gripped the Olympic bar, and I took a deep breath in and out as I lifted the bar off of the resting place and up above my chest. Breathing in deep, I lifted the bar before gradually allowing it to come closer to my chest. Pushing out an exhalation, I pushed the bar up once more. I did three sets of ten before putting the bar back on the resting spot. Sitting up, I grabbed the towel to wipe my face. Resting my face in the soft fabric, I breathed in the fresh scent of linen.

One of the many good things about Christina being in my life was now I had the softest towels on the planet. We both had our own household essentials, but according to Christina, my towels and blankets were not salvageable in the move. Back when we had packed up my home during the move to the apartment, she had picked up one of my towels and asked with a hand on her hip, "What in the heck is this monstrosity?" She had waved the towel in the air.

At the time, I had been packing up a box from my bedroom. "Uh… A towel?"

"No, it's a piece of sandpaper. Are all your linens like this?" She had rifled through the cabinet where I had kept my towels and extra blankets. Her hand had felt up all the pieces of fabric, and with each one she had touched, she had thrown them over her shoulder. "These all hafta go, Teddy. I'll be getting ya real towels."

"'Real towels'?" I had smirked, my shoulders shook as I had chuckled. "Are those not real enough? They do a pretty decent job to me. I always came out of the bathroom dry afterward."

She had clicked her tongue and had rolled her eyes. "No, Teddy. It ain't. These are rough-as-rocks towels. You're livin' with me now, and I'll be getting ya real towels. Ones that are soft like a baby…" She had lifted another towel, which was crinkled and stuck to its lazy folded position I had put it in. She had scowled in disgust. "And fabric softener." On that day a year ago, seeing her all worked up about the towels had made me fall for her a little more. She had left down the stairs. "New, fresh towels!" she had yelled. Quieter to herself, though, I heard her mumble, "This boy, I cannot believe he has been livin' like some caveman…"

Looking back on that memory made me laugh as I continued with my workout. Today was my first time lifting a hundred pounds. I had been working my way up to that weight, and it was not easy. By the final set, my arms were shaking as I struggled to push the bar up. Afterward, I did pull ups, and after the twentieth one, my upper arms burned. When I finished working out my arms, I focused on my upper back by using the dumbbells to build up the muscle.

Now done with weights, I ran on the treadmill for fifteen minutes, followed by two minutes of a slow jog. Sweat trickled down the side of my temples. After my workout, I headed back to my apartment to shower and get ready for work.

Taking off my workout shirt, I managed to ring out the sweat into the sink. Working out was a nasty business, but already I felt better. I rested my head against the tiled wall in the shower as the cool water beat onto my neck and back. My body heat lowered, and I breathed out in relief.

Once I finished, I decided to eat a light lunch before work. To the right of the bathroom was the kitchen and living room that was connected. The apartment was decent sized, but still no comparison to the house from a year ago. I opened our fridge to take out some spinach. Above our stove was a cabinet where I kept some hemp seeds and protein powder. Mixing up the ingredients with some water, I put it in the blender. I grabbed an apple from the basket on our round kitchen table and took a seat to eat my lunch before heading off to work.

Being alone at the table gave me time to think, which wasn't good. Often, my thoughts went straight to my nightmares which were centered around the house. Last night's dream was of me running in the mountains trying to look for my mom. In the dream, I was in the same mountains where my parents' cabin was. In the same woods where my mother first got taken by Dr. Ransteen two years ago. I couldn't find her anywhere in the dream, but in the middle of the street stood Dr. Ransteen. He was covered in blood, and for some reason I knew it had to be my mother's blood.

And that's what I woke up to on this fine morning— in a cold sweat and trying to catch my breath.

Enough eating. I have to go before my mind continues to think. On days like this I looked forward to clocking in for work because it served as a distraction. Once I clocked in, I checked on my first patient, Mr. Foster. As a certified nursing assistant at a skilled nursing facility, it was my job to help oversee a number of patients. Mr. Foster was new to the program, and he wasn't too happy about being here. He and I had that in common. Each day, I made sure to bring him a peach from the cafeteria to cheer him up. "Thanks, Ted," he said as he took hold of my small gift. "It'd be nice if they had a tennis court here for us," said Mr. Foster in his shaky voice. His hand wobbled uncontrollably as he lifted the peach towards his mouth. He bit into it and took a while to chew it.

"How are you today?" I asked as I fluffed the pillow behind him.

He sighed as he stared at his peach. "I grew the best peaches in town. Better than this, in fact. I should have my granddaughter come by to give you a bundle of them."

I grimaced at the kind gesture. "She still running the farm for you?"

"Yeah," he said with a somewhat disappointed tone. He pursed his lips. "I miss it there, but I also miss tennis."

"Tennis could be dangerous. Especially with your recent hip injury."

He waved his hand dismissively. "My children worry too much."

I stood in front of him and eyed him up and down. "You fell while working on the farm. That's serious."

He scowled. "Feels like a punishment to be old since I'm stuck in here now." His voice rose. "Why am I being punished?"

I grimaced. "They are just trying to do what's best for you."

He took another bite and spoke with his mouth full. Juice seeped from his lips. "No, it's so they don't have to keep an eye on me so they can go about their lives." He pointed at me and said, "Don't you ever do that to your folks. Ya hear me?"

I sighed as I thought of my mother, and I blinked away the tears that threatened to seep out. "No, sir. I would never think of it."

He sat back against the now fluffed pillows on his bed. "Good."

After checking in with Mr. Foster, I left to check on the next patient. Working half days was all I could muster, and to be honest, it wasn't just the grief. My sneakers squeaked against the shiny tile in the hallway. I looked down at the floor as the light from the ceiling reflected off the ground. The retirement home had a way of smelling like antiseptic mixed with Bengay, and it was my first time noticing. It was also beginning to bother me.

My coworker, Ben, came by with a hand raised, and I lifted mine for the high-five we always gave one another. "How goes it, Ted?" he asked. He clicked his pen nonstop as he chewed his gum. On the left pocket of his scrubs was Monica's pen with a black ribbon tied around it. Seeing it always sent a stir through me because I was there to find her charred body in the firepit Dr. Ransteen burned her in. Ben carries his grief well, but I knew under all that charisma and humor was someone hurting.

I shrugged. "It's been an alright morning."

"Okay, good." He smiled, but it didn't reach his eyes. His smile hasn't been the same since Monica's funeral. At the time, I had no idea how close he and Monica had become. They dated when she was alive, but Ben apparently fell in love with her. "I thought with the news of the demolishment you'd be a little bit out of sorts."

Ben didn't know much about what took place. Christina was the only one that knew every detail of the incident. Ben only knew what the cops knew, which was that Howard tried to kill my mother and me, minus the spirit possession and occult stuff.

I shook my head.

Keep it in the box.

"No, I'm good. The past is the past," I said.

Ben smiled real big as he clasped a hand onto my shoulder. His eyes still dead inside. "Good! Well, I'm off on my rounds. Catch up with you soon." As he walked away, he turned around and said, "I thought you'd be interested in that secret room they found, at least."

I stopped in my tracks. My stomach dropped as I turned to face him. "Secret room?"

Ben stopped walking backward. "Yeah, man. The construction workers found some secret room in the basement. It's all over the news. After they took down part of the cemented wall in the basement, it revealed a sealed room. It's got a bunch of crap in it, apparently." He titled his head to one side. "You okay?"

I swallowed before realizing I had stopped breathing. "Y-yeah."

Ben sounded suspicious. "Ooo-kay, 'cause you're pale as fuck right now."

I tried to calm my heartrate by taking big, slow breaths. "I-is the house demolished yet?"

He shook his head. "I drove by it on my way to work this morning; they are still just taking out the windows and some of the walls. They paused since they found the secret room. They are waiting until some historian can come by to get the stuff."

I managed a nod. "Thanks."

"I mean it, Ted. You good?" He furrowed his brow.

I swallowed and straightened my posture. "Yeah. S-sure. Talk to you later."

Ben didn't seem convinced, but he didn't dig any further and instead waved at me before turning around and heading down the hall. When nobody was looking, Ben would hang his head low, but I saw.

The box, Ted. Remember the box.

I went about my day as usual and tried to push the thoughts of the secret room to the back of my mind. However, no matter how hard I tried, it poked at me relentlessly like an annoying pinprick. By the end of my shift, I had developed a headache. I took my last ten-minute break in the employee lounge where Christina was. Plopping down on a chair, I hung my head against the backrest. Christina had just ended her shift an hour before mine was over. She dug through her huge purse for her keys as she spoke. "Hey, Teddy. I'm gonna pick up some dinner. I feel like Italian, so I wanted to ask ya what you wanted." She peered up at me, and her brow creased. "What's the matter, Teddy? You look whiter than a sheet." She put her hand to my forehead. "Ya feel clammy. Don't tell me you're catchin' a cold."

I took a breath out. "They found a hidden room."

"What?" she asked, confused.

I closed my eyes and pinched the bridge of my nose. "The construction workers were doing the demolishment. They found a hidden room." I opened my eyes to see Christina had put a hand to her mouth.

It was silent for a moment.

Christina gave a nod. "Okay." She said "okay" again with more determination. "Do you want to go there to see it?" She put her hand on top of mine. "Is that something you need?"

I looked away from her. "I don't know. I just want to forget."

13

"I think…" Christina paused, "ya should go and take a look. You never got closure, Teddy. Ya owe yourself that much, hon." She smoothed her hand over mine and up my arm. I closed my eyes again as I let her touch soothe me.

I disagreed with her. There was nothing at that house I needed closure on. I'd had a traumatic event happen there and that was it. Why revisit it? Shaking my head some more, I said, "No. It'll just open old wounds."

I could tell Christina wanted to say more by how she pressed her lips tightly together. She sighed. "Fine. Okay. We won't go, but if you eva' change ya mind, that's okay."

Grounding my teeth together, my chest became hot from anger. It wasn't like me to get so agitated by someone's concern, but I just took it as pity from her, which squashed my pride.

After the residents ate their dinner, I made my rounds in each room, delivering their medication. "Here you go, Mr. Foster," I said as I handed him the small paper cup that had his pain medication.

"Thanks," he said.

Putting my hands in my scrubs' pockets, I asked, "You need anything else before I head out?"

"No book this time for me?" he asked.

My eyes widened in surprise. "I forgot. I'm sorry. Do you want me to go grab it?"

He flipped his hand dismissively. "Nah, go home."

I would have insisted before, but I was tired today. At this point, I just wanted to go home. Once I clocked out, I sat in my truck, waiting for the heater to kick on some more as I rubbed my hands together. My phone vibrated in my pocket.

When I checked the caller ID, it was my sister. My chest tightened, and I hesitated as I clicked to accept the call.

"Hey, Scarlett," I said with a sigh.

"Okay, where have you been?" Right to business, as always. Her tone was short.

I pinched the bridge of my nose. "I've been busy."

"What the hell is wrong with *you*? You sound like shit."

Usually, her rough demeanor would make me laugh, but not today. "Nothing," I snapped.

My tone didn't falter her. "It sure doesn't sound like nothin'," she said. She sighed. "What's going on? Seriously. I've hardly heard from you since last year's Thanksgiving brawl."

I lifted an eyebrow. "Brawl?"

"Yeah! That's what *I'm* calling it."

That heat bubbled to the surface again, and I ground my teeth together. "I only hit him once," I said.

"He's still your dad, though. You don't punch your parents."

"He isn't my dad," I paused. "Not anymore."

"Oh. My. God. You are being overdramatic, and I thought *I* was the girl."

Putting my hand into a fist, I said quickly, "I gotta go."

"I miss you," she said quietly in a softer tone.

"Yeah. Bye." Hanging up, I slammed my phone into the passenger seat. I let out a sharp sigh and rested my head on the steering wheel. My head reeled back to that Thanksgiving evening with my now alcoholic father. Just thinking about his face made me punch the steering wheel. I drove for a while to cool off before heading home.

Once I got to the apartment, Christina was setting out the to-go boxes from the Italian restaurant, along with some forks. I walked over to greet her with a kiss. "What'll ya be drinking, hon?" she asked me.

"Water is fine," I said taking a seat at our small round table. It wasn't made out of real wood. It was some kind of synthetic material with a painted-on wood design. The paint was beginning to fade. There were stab marks from a fork on one end which were done by me.

After the house three years ago, I was a nervous wreck. At the time, I hadn't even noticed I had been stabbing at the table with my fork during dinner until Christina had pointed it out to me. We had just moved in together, and the nightmares had been constant. Any sudden noise had set me on edge. I hadn't told her entirely what had happened until that first night after moving into the apartment. I'd needed to get it off my chest or I'd explode. That and she'd deserved to know what she was getting herself into.

As reluctant as I had been, I had been so emotionally depleted I didn't care if she had left me or not. I had begun the sentence with, "This is going to sound crazy, and you are going to leave right out that door once I say it, which is fine."

Her brow had furrowed, and she had said softly, "Ted—"

"Let me finish." I had let out a breath. "Please."

She had sat up straight and nodded.

My mouth had stayed open as I had thought of what to say. "I... It's..." I'd sighed. "Okay, so everything that happened to me wasn't normal. At first, I didn't believe what was going on with me, and I wanted more than anything to make sense of it. Remember how I told you I had dreams about Monica's sister Lavinia? And we were investigating her murder, and then her killer, Howard, took the evidence from my home and started stalking Monica?"

Christina had nodded. "And he…" she'd swallowed, "killed Monica."

I had nodded. "Well, there is more to the story than that. Much more." I had taken a deep breath. "Okay, here it goes… I saw ghosts and got attacked by things I didn't even believe existed, and I assumed it was stress or some kind of mental illness. I swear, the last thing I believed was it was all real, but when Monica got involved, it became too much for me to keep denying. Howard was…" I had chewed on the inside of my cheek as I had debated telling her. "Howard wasn't Howard anymore. He didn't kill Lavinia. It was some spirit who possessed him and who had previously owned that house. The spirit's name was Dr. Ransteen." I had eyed Christina warily to see her reaction.

Instead of meeting me with suspicion or judgment, her whole body had leaned over the table, and she had grabbed ahold of my hand. Her eyes, wide with enthrallment, had bored into mine. Her reaction had helped to push me to continue.

I had continued to chew on the inside of my cheek. "There was some kind of occult thing Dr. Ransteen had involved himself in when he was alive because he wanted to be immortal. I would get visions in dreams about his rituals, and he would take possession of someone who was alive to continue the work he had started."

17

"What work?" Christina had scooted her seat closer. It was as if she had been told some kind of entertaining, spooky story. I hadn't been sure if I liked that reaction.

"He was doing illegal experiments on his patients in order to cure mental illnesses that were otherwise permanent. He ran a mental hospital in that mansion when he was alive, and nobody else had lived there until Lavinia and Howard moved in, and..." I had reeled off knowing Christina had now connected the dots starting from Lavinia and Howard, moving into the eventual possession of Howard.

Christina had furrowed her brow. "So you were trying to stop Howard from...?"

"We were trying to solve the murder, but that's when we learned Howard was involved, and he was killing all those mentally ill homeless people that were on the streets and doing experiments on them to continue his work. He didn't want us to stop him."

Christina had sat back in her chair.

"And my mother got picked up by him when she ventured away from the cabin up in the mountains. The possessed Howard took her to the mansion. I fought him, and the house got burned. Howard was arrested, but..."

Christina had crossed her arms as she blinked numerous times. I had learned she did that when she was thinking. "Howard wasn't the actual killer. It was Dr. Ransteen who had possessed him."

"Yeah," I had said slowly. "I know it's hard to believe, and I was going to just leave it alone and let you only know what the cops knew, but with us having moved in together, I figured it was time to tell you the whole truth. You deserve to know what you're getting yourself into." I

18

had laughed lightly as I had run my fingers through my hair. "A crazy man who… may or may not believe in ghosts."

It had been silent, and I had refused to meet Christina's eyes in fear of what I'd see there. Judgment? Fear? Acceptance? It had taken the touch of Christina's hand on my arm to get me to finally gaze up at her. "Teddy," she had said softly. The look in her eyes was something I had not recognized. "I know that must have been hard to tell me, so thank you. I believe…" She had gone quiet for a minute and did that blinking thing she did. "I believe you experienced what ya did, because you are not someone to make somethin' up like that. I know you. I may not understand it fully, but I'm willin' to accept your experience as yours."

Well, that wasn't the response I had wanted. I hadn't been sure what I had wanted, to be honest. Her to believe me wholeheartedly? Then again, I hadn't thought I'd like to be with someone who'd believe in this crap right off the bat. I had preferred someone with some sense of grounded thinking. We had left it at that. Christina had known about the nightmares, so she knew how the event had affected me. She had been supportive of my healing process.

I blinked away the memory of that night when we first moved into our apartment and looked up from the tiny craters the fork had left behind on our table.

Christina was right: I might need to go to the house to check out that secret room, but there was this wave of fear that swam through my gut. It twisted and churned, which made me lose my appetite for dinner. What if something happened to me by revisiting the house? What if somehow there was some spirit there that would attack me?

I let out a big breath and shook my head. "Let's eat," I said, wanting to distract myself. Despite my appetite being gone, I forced the spaghetti into my mouth to not worry Christina. She always worried whenever I didn't eat or whenever I didn't shower, brush my teeth, or do anything to take care of myself. It was endearing but annoying when she felt the need to care for me. I was so used to taking care of others, it was new being on the receiving end of it.

After dinner, we cuddled on the couch as we watched television. I wasn't looking forward to sleeping because that's when the dreams came.

They always came.

Twirling Christina's hair with my fingers, she looked up at me with a small smile. "Don't be nervous," she said, grabbing at my fingers. "I'm here. I'll wake you up if anything happens, okay?"

I gnawed at the inside of my cheek.

"Do you want to take some of my anxiety meds before bed?"

I shook my head. "I don't need it. I just need to relax, is all."

Christina grimaced before kissing my cheek. "Okay, hon."

When we finally went to bed, I lay there staring up at the ceiling as I clutched at the sheets hoping for at least one night of some good rest. I reluctantly did some deep breathing exercises to calm my nerves.

Take a deep breath in. Hold for three seconds. Then breathe out and hold for three seconds.

I felt foolish for having to do this. A man should be able to sleep just fine without the need for a meditation, but here I was—in bed, unable to do the simplest of tasks without having a damn heart attack. Despite my efforts, a nightmare came as always.

*

My mother sat tied to a wooden chair in the damp, cemented basement of the mansion. It was dark and murky as always. The sound of a loose pipe dripped in the back. "Ted!" she called out. "Ted! Where am I? Help me! Where are you?" I was standing right there, but she couldn't see me. Her eyes darted around the room in search of me.

"I'm right here, Mom!" I yelled as I got closer to her right in front of her face. I could see the sweat that dripped down her face. The wrinkles that lined her mouth and eyes were constricted with fear.

"Ted!" she yelled. "Where are you?"

"I'm right here!" I wanted to grab her, but I had no arms. It was as if my body wasn't there at all, despite me being able to see and hear. I spoke in hushed tones, "Mom, relax. I'll find some way to get to you. Just stay quiet so he doesn't find you."

"Where are you? Where am I? Ted! Ted!" she kept yelling. I implored her to stay quiet, but it was as if she couldn't hear me. The sound of footsteps crunching at each step told me he was here. Dr. Ransteen always appeared the same in my dreams: mid-forties with graying hair along the side of his brown hair. His menacing face was long and square shaped. He was clean-shaven with bright blue eyes this time, though. He wore a white lab coat that reached to his ankles.

Adrenaline shot through my body making my feet tingle. Quickly, I turned to my mother and screamed, "Mom!

21

Get out now!" Right then, a bright blaze appeared to the right. It exploded across the room, making everything turn bright orange as my mother's hair singed and her face melted from the flames.

I shot awake in bed with a gasp. A cool sweat beat down my face and chest. Christina stirred awake. "Mm... Hey," she mumbled. She groaned as she turned over. Her curly hair had this way of becoming a rat's nest full of frizz and knots, and the hilarious sight of it helped to ease my tense mood a bit. She sat herself up and put a hand on my shoulder. "You okay? Another nightmare, hon?"

I took a deep breath. "Yeah."

She kissed my shoulder and then my cheek before wrapping her arms around me. Leaning her head against one of my shoulders, she said, "Need a cup of water or something?"

I shook my head. "No, I'm fine." Getting up, I walked out of our bedroom to the bathroom. I splashed water on my face; the cold water helped shock the fear out of me. Drying my face with a towel, I took a deep breath. In the mirror, I saw my bloodshot eyes debating whether I should just watch television or attempt to sleep again. The bed won, and I crawled back under the covers.

I chewed on my bottom lip as I closed my eyes and tried to force myself asleep. After several minutes, I shot them open again and let out an exasperated sigh. Turning over, I counted the clock's hand on my nightstand before my eyelids got heavy and I eventually fell asleep.

Another day at work was like a blur. As much as I enjoyed seeing my patients' smiles, the job itself was grueling. By grueling, I meant not fulfilling. At least not like it used to be, but I refused to quit and give up on my patients. "I love my job. I love my job. I love my job," I mumbled under my breath as I made my way to the cafeteria to pick up Mr. Foster's lunch. Some days he couldn't bring himself to get up because of his sore hip, so I did it for him. The cafeteria was large and smelt of ketchup and waffles with burnt syrup. We had about twelve round tables with enough seats to fit about half of our residents. It was more than enough since half of the residents couldn't make their way to the cafeteria at all. Near the cafeteria's entrance was the opening to the kitchen where the lunch trays were handed out over a metal counter. Large windows on one side of the wall allowed you to look out towards the outside patio area with a sliding glass door. I sighed as I picked up the tray of food. "You good?" asked my coworker, Carlos. He stood next to me, picking up a fresh apple from the produce basket at the end of the metal counter.

"Just tired," I said as I grabbed some utensils. Today's lunch was soup with half a sandwich. The soup itself appeared to be made of mostly water with a few carrot chunks.

"You're always tired," said Carlos with worry in his voice, which made my irritation spike. "You haven't gone out to the bar or nothin' for a while now. We were planning on heading out tonight." Carlos smiled to appear more inviting. "Bring Christina along."

I licked my lips and let out a heavy breath. "Can't. I have a thing to do."

Carlos clicked his tongue. "Yeah. I get it." His tone seemed short.

My muscles tensed as I gripped onto the food tray. "No, you don't," I said as I shoved past him out of the cafeteria. Letting Carlos get to me like that was unlike me, and I knew it was only because he missed his friend, but it was like I couldn't control my anger at that moment.

Storming off, I passed the employee restroom and could hear someone crying.

I paused.

The clear sound of Ben's cries melted away the unwarranted fury. He always cried during his break, and it hadn't let up. Softly, I knocked on the door. "Hey, Ben..."

He sniffed before opening the door and said, "Hey, man!" Smiling, he tried to hide the pain in his soaked eyes. "Can't a guy go to the bathroom in peace around here?" He patted my shoulder, and before I could speak, he hurried past me and down the hall.

Part of me wanted to be there for Ben more, but I was far too preoccupied dealing with my own demons.

After work, I came home to the fresh scent of bacon. Christina was busying herself with preparing dinner. "I thought of making a cobb salad tonight with bacon." The sight of the bag of spinach in her hands sparked memories of my mother. She'd say, "Ain't nothing wrong with a little bacon. Just as long as you balance it out with something healthy like spinach." We'd have spinach and bacon all the time. It was her way of "cheating" a diet.

The remembrance of my mother further fueled my agitation from earlier. "I'm not hungry," I growled before stomping off to our bedroom and slamming the door shut. Sitting on the edge of the bed, I yanked at the ends of my hair. I hated more than anything how angry I was for no reason, but it was as if I couldn't control it. It made me frustrated on top of that, so I punched at the mattress to help relieve my tension.

On days like these, I spent the evening in the bedroom watching YouTube videos because I didn't want to lash out at Christina. A phone call interrupted one of my videos. It was my therapist. Chewing on my tongue, I debated whether or not I wanted to answer it. I let it go to voicemail, but he called again soon after.

I decided to answer. "What?" I breathed out.

"How are you doing today?" asked Dr. Whitaker.

"Fine."

"Are you sure about that?"

I heard the television from the living room had been turned off suddenly. Peering down at the bottom of the bedroom door, I saw shadows of feet. Christina was listening in. She must've called. Having been caught, I decided to fess up. "Today was rough. I had another nightmare."

"What was it this time?"

"My mother was stuck in the basement, and then it caught on fire. I saw *him* again."

"Uh-huh… Have you been doing your relaxation exercises before bed like I've asked you to?"

I rubbed my eyes and shoved down the annoyance that knotted in my chest. "No."

"What about your journal where I asked you to document your feelings and the triggers? Have you been doing that?"

I let out an exasperated sigh. "No."

"You'll never get better unless you heed my advice." He sounded like a father disciplining his son for breaking grandma's expensive vase.

"I know," I said through gritted teeth.

"I'm going to refer you to a psychiatrist. Your moods seem to be getting worse, and you refuse to accept help from me. You don't have to take anything prescribed by the psychiatrist, but I encourage you to listen to what he or she has to say," said Dr. Whitaker.

"I'm not crazy," I exclaimed.

"I didn't say you were," Dr. Whitaker said in an all-too-calm tone.

"I don't need meds," I defended.

"Medicine helps facilitate an easier healing process. It doesn't have to be a permanent solution. Therapy accompanied by medicine can help you better and faster."

I was silent as I chewed on my tongue, not wanting to yell at him. How many times did I need to put my foot down about this?

"I'll have someone call you. Just listen to what the doctor has to say and then decide. All I ask is that you listen."

Rubbing my face, I said in a short tone, "Fine."

"Okay. You take care. I'll see you at our next appointment."

Once our call was done, I threw my phone onto the bed. I felt like such a child throwing a temper tantrum, but I couldn't help myself. It made my stomach twist in anger at how pathetic I was acting, but it was as if I was a puppet on a string. There was no control on my end. All I had was this beast called anger.

That night, another dream came; this time, it was an aerial view of the plot of land on which the house once stood.

It was gone.

The only thing that remained was the cemented basement. It was perfectly intact except for one side of it. I flew in closer and saw a rusty red door made of metal behind the broken wall. Voices whispered through the air, but I couldn't make out what they were saying. After a while, one voice broke out amongst the others. She sounded familiar, but I couldn't place her. "The papers. There are books," the voice said.

"More is to come," the voice whispered close to my ear.

"More is coming. *It* is coming. You need the books."

The rest of the voices got louder and louder, shrouding over the woman's, before I felt a shove towards the door. The shock of my body being slammed into the door woke me up yet again.

Panting, I ran fingers through my hair. Hearing about the secret room was now causing a whole new set of dreams, apparently. Christina was right. I had to go back to the house. I thought of what the mysterious woman had said, and a chill ran down my spine. Who and what was "it"? Maybe going would make the nightmares disappear somehow. It seemed like a stretch, but I was desperate as I let out a sharp breath. I didn't want to do this, but there was this unknown force that gnawed at the back of my brain, which told me I had to go.

Thankful I didn't wake Christina this time, I carefully pulled the covers off of me and steadily got out of the bed, making sure I didn't make any sudden movements so as not to wake her. I tiptoed out of the room and closed the door behind me before making my way to the couch to distract myself with some television.

I didn't even notice how much time had passed until a soft orange color from the sun broke through the living room area's curtains and painted across the carpet. The sweet aroma of the beans filled my nostrils and helped ease the exhaustion a bit as I made myself a cup of coffee. I made sure to leave some left over for Christina when she eventually woke up.

Closer to Christina's alarm going off, I decided to begin making breakfast— omelets filled with spinach, bell pepper, onion, cheese, and bacon. I smirked as I remembered my mother's old saying, "A little bit of bacon never hurt." Immediately, a heavy ache weighed down on my chest, and I let out a sigh to shove away the grief.

Christina's alarm blared behind the bedroom door, and moments later the door squeaked open. She came out while putting on her robe. Her hair was in disarray as she shuffled to the coffee pot. "Good morning, babe," I said.

"Ugh," she groaned in return.

She was adorable in the morning. Chuckling, I patted my hand on her rat's nest to fix some of the knots. "I have breakfast ready for you," I said, flipping over the omelet.

Christina took a sip of her coffee, and her eyes opened up a little more. "Mm-hmm."

She sat down at the kitchen table and laid her head on it. A minute later, she lifted her head to take a sip from her mug before slamming her forehead on the table. I brought over her plate along with mine. The smell of the food lifted her head once more, and she grabbed the fork in her fist.

Figuring now was as good a time as any to tell her my mind had changed, I cleared my throat. "I decided to go to the house."

Christina had a slight pause after she took a bite of her food. She nodded. "Good," she grumbled.

I eyed her carefully to see her reaction, but it seemed neutral despite her grumpy morning mood. "I'll go tonight by myself."

Christina shook her head. She rubbed her hands over her face, which made her eyes wake up fully. "No, I'm comin' with." She patted my hand. "And we gotta dress in all black and sneak over that fence like undercover cops." Her lazy morning smile made a grin spread across my face.

I reached out to kiss her hand. "Kids have been breaking onto the property and vandalizing it. I'm pretty sure a couple of thirty-somethings can manage a slick break-in," I smirked.

Christina giggled. "And we'd be better at it." She pointed her fork at me. "More experience."

I chuckled. "True."

After breakfast, Christina got ready for work. Again, she had the morning shift while I had the afternoon one. Making myself busy, I cleaned up the kitchen and got our dirty clothes ready for a load of laundry before heading off to work. I needed to keep myself busy because the consecutive nightmares were weighing heavily on my mind.

Before heading out the door, Christina kissed my cheek. She held my face in her hands and stared me straight in the eye. "Don't forget to breathe. It's gon' all be okay. I promise." Her smile instilled trust in me. Nodding my head, I let out a slow breath. Being vulnerable around Christina was still fresh, but I felt safe around her. It was a new concept for me to feel safe around someone emotionally because I didn't exactly have that as a child. My father instilled in me the need to be strong and "like a man," which meant not crying. No emotions. However, I was growing to like the sheltered bubble Christina had made for me. For the first time in my life, I could breathe. She gave me my breath.

At work, I saw Carlos leisurely pushing one of our metal carts along, which had books stacked on them. One of the nursing assistants did a book run every day to see if any of the residents wanted to read something.

Remorse yanked at my heart, so I made my way over to him. "Hey," I said with a grimace.

Carlos stopped in his tracks and lifted his eyebrows in surprise. "Hi."

I chewed on my lip as I tried to find the right words to say. "I'm sorry about yesterday. I…" I trailed off, trying to find the words. "There's no excuse."

Carlos nodded his head. "I'm just worried about you. We all are."

I peered down at the ground for a moment. "I know." I kicked at the linoleum flooring, which made my sneakers squeak. "I'm trying."

"I've been where you are before."

"Really?"

"Yeah," Carlos shrugged. "When my father was killed, I was angry for a long time. There was no justice for him either, and I was there to watch him die."

I stood there with my eyes widened in dismay. "I had no idea."

Carlos sighed. "Yeah, well, I don't like talking about it much. It took years of therapy to get where I'm at today, but I first had to accept the fact I needed the help." His eyes studied mine. "Refusing the help will only make it worse. There's nothing wrong with a little help now and again."

Looking away, I sucked in a breath. "They want me on meds."

"Then you should take them. I did."

"Seriously?"

Carlos shrugged again. "Yeah. It was only for a year, and now I don't need them. Some people need it permanently, but I was lucky enough to be okay without it. Sometimes we fall. It's okay to fall. It's okay to be human," Carlos grimaced. "You're a man. Not an invincible creature without emotions." Carlos continued to roll past me. He patted my shoulder as he did so. "You'll get there." His eyes were sincere. "I'm here if you need me."

His understanding and honesty released a heaviness within me I didn't notice I had. It allowed me to swallow my pride and be willing to accept help. Maybe it was something I could tell Ben too, but I didn't see him at all that day. During my break, I tried calling him, but it all went straight to voicemail.

I hope he's okay.

After my shift was over, I left to the apartment where Christina was busying herself with putting together our supplies for the night: two backpacks, flashlights, gloves, and a first aid kit. I couldn't help but smile. "A first aid kit, Christina?" I asked her playfully.

She looked at me as if she didn't find it silly at all that she was overprepared. "Yes. Ya never know what'll happen."

I put my keys and wallet on the side table near the front door. "Heaven forbid I scrape a knee." I turned over my shoulder to let her see my grin so she'd know I was only teasing.

She sighed before laughing. "Yeah, yeah. One day you will thank me for it… Since it isn't sundown yet, we can eat dinner or somethin'."

I shrugged. My appetite still hadn't returned, but I didn't want to worry her. "I had a big lunch," I lied. "I'm not hungry just yet."

Christina nodded. She fit her lips into a tight line and said, "Carlos told me about your talk today and what happened yesterday."

Grounding my teeth together, I bit back the sudden fury that burned in my chest. Why it made me so upset Carlos and Christina were speaking about me, I had no idea. I crossed my arms.

Christina was quiet as she studied me with her eyes. "We're worried. That's all," she said softly.

I stared up at her. "Drop it," I said through gritted teeth. "I'm fine."

Christina's brow furrowed. She swallowed as she looked me up and down. "Okay," she said in a sassy tone. We got ready to take off to the old house in silence.

I didn't think I'd be nervous about going back to the property, but as the sunlight along our carpet began to turn a faint pink color, I couldn't ignore the churning in my stomach. I told myself it was because of our adventure's breaking-and-entering component, but deep down, I knew it was more than that. Chewing on the inside of my cheek, my knee shook as I sat at the table. Every few minutes, I'd get up and pace around.

Christina peered up from the lounge chair in the living room where she sat crocheting. "Teddy, hon?"

I paused. "Yeah?"

"You 'kay?" She tilted her head to one side.

Nodding, I took a deep breath to help shovel down the emotions. "Yeah. I'm good."

Christina raised her eyebrows as if she didn't believe me. "Mm-hmm."

By nightfall, we were dressed and ready to go. Drumming my fingers against my thighs, I stood there waiting for Christina to lock our apartment door. We made our way downstairs to the bottom floor and out the wooden door that had a glass window attached to the top of it. Christina was parked across the way. She had an electric car, and it still threw me off how silent it was whenever she turned it on.

I played with my sweatshirt hood once we'd made our way across town to the old house. I hadn't been back to that place since I sold it. It seemed strange to be back there suddenly.

They had ripped out the bushes and flowers that used to sit out along the front entrance. A chain-link fence now circled the property. They had placed that up after the last owner left. He wasn't able to sell it, so the bank took over. Nobody dared buy the property; despite being on the market for almost a year now, not one person came to look at it.

The windows that used to be boarded up were now gone, having been bashed in by the construction workers. I could see through the empty window frames that some of the walls had been torn down. The home used to have every window and door boarded up in order to deter the teens from breaking and entering at night. Graffiti sat on one side of the house, and I could see from the moonlight there was more graffiti inside the kitchen.

In the dark, with part of the house having been stripped away, it didn't seem as menacing as my mind had made it out to be.

"Ready, Teddy?" Christina asked. She placed a hand on my knee, which I didn't even notice was shaking.

I took a deep breath. *Get yourself together, Ted. This isn't a big deal. It's just a house at night.* There was a sense of frustration with myself for being so unmanly by fearing an inanimate object such as this building. I fear only the idea of it and what took place here and nothing else. I'd faced death there. Anyone would be frightened to face their mortality again. That's what I told myself as I stepped out of the car. All I needed was to go in and out. If kids could break in and do God-knows-what there, then I could come in to check out a measly room.

Christina put her hood on over her head and gave me a backpack. "Don't turn on the flashlight until we get in," she said. I helped her hop the fence first by letting her jump off my hands, and then I climbed over. The metal clanked and shook as my weight made it unsteady. Once I reached the top, I leaped down to the ground. Christina and I walked up the porch, half of which had been dismantled. The wood steps groaned with each step we took. The previous owner took out the railway Christina and I had built together. It made my heart sink that I never realized my dream of caring for my mother in this home.

Christina leaped onto the windowsill that led to the living room before crawling inside through the exposed window frame. I did the same. Once inside, we turned on the flashlights to see. "We have to hurry just in case the patrol car comes by to check," said Christina.

Dust and crumbles of what once was a wall were sprinkled across the cemented floor. They had taken out the linoleum, floorboards, and staircase. The inside of the home seemed to have aged more from the outside elements' exposure after the windows were taken out. Our feet shuffled across the living room, and something from the upper floor creaked loudly, making us halt in our tracks.

Christina eyed me as we both paused to listen for another sound. When nothing happened after several seconds, we continued our pursuit. We made our way to the basement entrance, where the stairs used to be. The door to the basement had been taken out, so all that was left was the doorframe. The black abyss greeted us at the opening was threatening. My heart rate sped up a bit, but I managed to push it back.

It's just a house. It's just the memory you are afraid of.

Christina grabbed ahold of my hand and squeezed lovingly. That small contact was enough to make everything melt away. With some newfound bravery, I used my flashlight to guide my way down the steps. The air was silent. Not even the wind broke through. The world outside seemed to cease to exist as total silence enveloped our ears.

Not even a car could be heard. It was as if being in the basement transported us to another dimension.

With my ears ringing, we scuffled across the cemented floor of the basement. My heart stopped, and a cold sweat ran down my spine. In front of me was a big gash where a wall once stood. Chunks of the cemented wall lay on the floor beside it. Behind the hole was a rusty red door.

Just like in my dream.

I clenched my teeth, saying the same lie over and over in my head: *It's just a house. It was just a dream. It is just a coincidence.*

Christina decided to climb over the side of the hole in the wall with me frozen in place. She managed to get one leg over but needed my help with the other. My feet were like jelly as I made my way over the open cavity in the wall. Nearly tripping over the rubble, it caused a spike in my adrenaline to shoot up my spine. I took a deep breath to collect myself. Christina turned the rectangular handle, and the metal door screeched as it opened.

Our flashlights revealed a small room the size of a closet, which had two shelves filled with leather-bound books and loose papers.

"More is coming. It is coming. You need the books."

My breath caught in my throat. We walked into the room, and a musty scent bombarded my nostrils. I gingerly touched one of the books. Dust coated my fingertips, and I picked up the book and gently blew the dust off of it, which caused me to sneeze. The leather was soft and feeble with age. Christina and I eyed one another. We didn't need to say a word because she knew already we needed to take these. Christina went to work, shoving as much as she could into her backpack. She managed to fit two of the books into her backpack, and I grabbed the rest.

Christina had the flashlight in her mouth as she tried to speak, but everything came out a gargled mess. After filling up her backpack, she held the flashlight in her hand. "We need to get in and out as soon as possible."

"I know." I grabbed one of the red leather-bound books. The edge of its cover was fading, and some of its papers hung out loosely. Putting the yellow-colored papers and the last of the books into my backpack, we raced out of there. Despite the dream and everything I had experienced thus far, part of me, deep down, hoped nothing came of these papers and books. I knew we'd find something, but that only made me want to dig my head deeper into the ground rather than open that door to find out. I'd thought this part of my life was over. I *needed* it to be over; however, something gnawed at my heart. It made my stomach drop. There was something still there, and it cast a dark shadow around me at all times.

Chapter Two

Christina's Search

"I don't think I'll be able to sleep tonight," Ted said as he slammed open the apartment door. "We shouldn't have stolen those papers. It doesn't even matter what it says on them." I knew that was lie, but I knew he was just scared. He ran his fingers through his hair as he chewed on the inside of his cheek, which told me he was getting agitated.

"Teddy, hon," I implored, "it may be able to help with closure." I only wanted what was best for him and to help him let the past go. His nightmares happened every single night, and sometimes I pretended not to be woken up by them so as not to embarrass him. "I know ya hate how much I worry, but I only want to help," I said.

He ground his teeth together and paced back and forth in the living room. "I know!"

The rise in his voice made me take a step back.

Immediately, he sighed and closed his eyes. After a moment, he said in a calmer voice, "I'm sorry. The drive home from the house made me second guess our decision. I just…" He trailed off.

I knew he was on edge, but part of me wanted to settle this argument before doing anything else. "I'm worried about ya, Teddy. That's all, and I know there is more going on here because you are gettin' more irritated by the day. Don't close the door on unanswered questions that may haunt you."

He paused outside the bedroom door and banged his fist against the wall. Adrenaline rushed through me like a massive wave, and I took a big step back without thinking about it. "Just. Leave. It. Alone," he demanded through gritted teeth and slammed the bedroom door shut behind him. His words were garbled as he spoke, and the change in his voice made me frightened. His demand made me confused as well. Leave it alone? Leave what alone? It was as if a second person had jumped out to tell me this.

This wasn't like him. This wasn't my Teddy. It was like night and day. There was this thick air of anger that had surrounded him since we left that house earlier this evening. A part of me couldn't let this go. This needed to be resolved before anything else could happen, but he seemed to be at his limit. Pushing him any further would inevitably lead to an immense outburst.

I closed my eyes and took a deep and slow breath in and out in order to calm my pounding heart. Wanting to wait before I went back into the bedroom, I cleaned the kitchen for an hour. Keeping my hands busy helped to calm my nerves further. As I cleaned, I played the night over and over in my head. Slowly, as the night reeled in my mind, my concern turned into annoyance. My gut became hot with anger. Clenching my teeth together, I shook my head. I did *not* deserve to be treated like that. PTSD or not. Pushing the mop back and forth against the linoleum flooring, I continued to grind my teeth.

With the kitchen clean, I got myself ready for bed. I crawled into bed, making sure to be extra careful about not waking him. He turned over as I got under the covers and put an arm around my waist. The burning in my chest flared as I was reminded of how upset I was with him. "I'm sorry about how I was tonight," he mumbled.

That caught me off guard, and I didn't know what to say. "It wasn't okay, Teddy. I deserve better."

Ted smoothed his hand over my arm. "I know. You're right. There is no excuse." He was quiet for a second and then sighed. "Maybe the meds would help, but I don't want my suggesting that to suddenly make it okay for my behavior tonight. I'm not normally like this. I've been counting the number of days I've been irritable and on edge. It's every single day."

I thought for a moment. Irritability could be a number of things, but he was right he needed a psychiatrist at this point. "We'll make an appointment tomorrow," I suggested. "Seeing someone for medication doesn't mean what happened to you wasn't real. It doesn't mean you are crazy." Pausing, I mulled over if I should say this next or not. "As much as I love you," I began, unsure if I should continue, "I won't put up with abuse. I've been through that already, and—"

Ted pulled me closer to him, and my heart melted a little more. His face scrunched up in pain and sorrow. It made my heart drop. "I know," he whispered back. "I know, and I will do better. Just…" He paused as he gnawed on his lip. "If I say I have to leave and be alone, then don't ask any questions. Just let me go so I can decompress."

I nodded. "Okay. That's fair."

"At least until I get a hang on these mood swings."

Shaking my head, I said, "This isn't you, Teddy. I know you. This isn't it. What's happening?"

Ted swallowed, and a visible frown formed. His eyes widened in sudden fear, and his face became ashen. His expression sent a chill down my spine. "I don't know," he said with a shaky voice.

That night, I was woken up suddenly by the sounds of scratching. The time on my phone said it was one in the morning. I groaned, annoyed at the loud neighbors. Turning onto my back, I focused on the scraping. After a moment, I realized it didn't sound like the neighbors at all. Where was that coming from? Closing my eyes, I tried to get back to sleep. However, the scratching, like that of deep, heavy claws, kept going. The more it scratched, the heavier and louder it got. I shot open my eyes and sat up in bed.

What is that?

It sounded as though, whatever it was, was digging into a hard surface like wood. Ted was still fast asleep, so I got out of bed in search of its source. Nowhere in our apartment could I locate the sound. I opened our front door, and once I stepped out into the hallway, the sound ceased. Once back inside, the scraping continued.

We lived on the top floor, and there was no attic to my knowledge. Perhaps there was someone on the roof making this noise. I went back into bed but still sat up awake from the mysterious sound. At this point, I was becoming nervous. Was I imagining this? Picking at the hem of my blanket, I tried to take deep breaths in order to calm my rapid, beating heart.

The noise kept getting louder, and my nerves were so shot I decided to wake Ted up. "Teddy, hon," I whispered. He didn't stir awake, so I bent down lower towards his ear and called out his name.

Still no answer.

I grabbed his shoulder and shook him more aggressively. Right then, a menacing and deep growl reverberated in my ears. It was so close; I felt the heat of the unknown beast's breath on the back of my neck. I jumped out of bed with a scream. My stomach ached as it twisted and churned from my nerves. "Ted!" I screamed. "Wake up!" I ran over to his side of the bed and grabbed his arm as I started to shake him.

It was so unlike him to not wake up. Usually, he was such a light sleeper. "Ted!" I yelled.

Finally, he stirred awake. The second his eyes opened, and he saw mine, he sat up and grabbed my hand. "What's wrong? What happened?" he asked with clear panic in his voice. "You look so scared." He stroked the side of my face. The touch helped to calm me, but only a little.

"Th-there was…" I didn't know how to go about sharing what I experienced. "I heard scratchin'… I heard… a-a growl…" I fumbled with my fingers.

Ted looked into my eyes before grabbing me and holding me close to his chest. I wrapped my arms around him. The longer we embraced, the less my stomach felt acidic with nervousness.

I let out a sigh. "I don't know what that was. I want to say it was just a dream, but I was awake!" Blinking profusely, I thought back to what just happened. "I-I I know what I heard." I wanted him to believe me, but I was afraid he wouldn't. My eyes implored him.

Ted ran his fingers through my hair and said softly, "I know. I've experienced it too." He let out a sigh, which sounded like a relief. "This is how it started with me in that house before everything else started."

Swallowing hard, my eyes widened as my heart shot up to my throat. Now, this was happening to *me*? Ted was telling the truth. The thought of ghosts and goblins being real made my heart drop. I wasn't sure I wanted to live in a world where I knew this kind of evil existed. As Ted ran his hand up and down my back, I thought of the fear he must have lived with. No wonder he was on edge and short-tempered. I didn't care Ted didn't want closure. All I needed was this one experience to tell me things would only worsen if we didn't figure something out. Ted may not want the help, but I did.

I took the following day off from work. Last night's incident left me so exhausted, and my nerves were shot. I was mentally spent by sunrise, having spent the entire night staring up at the ceiling, too frightened to close my eyes. "Want me to stay home with you?" Ted asked as he stood near the front door, ready to leave.

Shaking my head, I faked a smile. Going over to him, I patted my hands on his chest. "No, hon. We both can't take the day off. We need the money."

Ted's strained face told me he disagreed with me, but before he could say anything, I turned him around and gently shoved him out the door. "Have a wonderful day, sweetie," I said. "I will be fine, dear. You'll be home before ya know it."

Being alone in that apartment was not something I wanted to do, but we had bills to pay, so one of us had to go to work. Besides, I had some homework to do on the house and needed to contact a friend I thought could help Ted. I turned on the television and raised the volume. The noise helped to soothe my apprehension, and I was finally able to breathe. In the bathroom, I dug through the cabinet beside the sink for my antidepressants. They also helped with anxiety symptoms.

Afterward, I got myself ready for the day to pass the time, since I knew my friend was probably still asleep at this hour. Busy hands always helped my anxiety. My hair was such a constant mess to deal with. It was curly, and the only thing I could use to tame it was an expensive leave-in conditioner. My mama always said good hair meant finding a good man. I pursed my lips at the silly thought of a woman's entire life being about finding some guy to marry.

Since it took me nearly two hours to get ready, it was late enough to give that old friend of mine a call by the time I was finished. I searched through my contacts on my phone until I found Jacob's name.

He picked up by the third ring. "Christina! Is that you? It has been too long," he said in his usual cheerful tone. Jacob's voice had a way of making you feel warm on the inside, and my frown quickly dissipated.

"Hey there, hon," I said. "I hope all is well with you and Deidre."

I could hear the smile in his voice. "It sure is. She and I just got back from a cruise to celebrate our anniversary."

"That must have been lovely. How long have y'all been together now? A century?" I giggled.

Jacob chuckled. "More like ten years. Not quite there yet, but here's to hopin'."

"Well, you got *me* to thank for introducing y'all. I knew her for those first few years in undergrad."

Jacob continued to laugh. "Yeah. I fell for her hard within seconds."

I had never believed in love at first sight until the moment when I'd witnessed that. Jacob had always been a hopeless romantic, though.

"I know you didn't call me to discuss my cruise," he said. "What's up?"

Gnawing on my lip, I paced back and forth in the kitchen. "I have a favor to ask, and I need your detective skills to help me solve somethin'."

Jacob cooed. "Shoot!"

His excitement made me a little braver. "As a history professor, I could use your expertise and finesse when it comes to an old case. Specifically in regards to the old mansion in town."

"You mean the one they are trying to demolish?"

"Yes. My boyfriend used to live there, and we got our hands on some old documents from the house I'd like for you to take a look at."

Jacob whistled. "That sounds just up my alley. Is it a cold case or something? I do love doing those in my spare time."

Shaking my head, I said, "I'm not sure if it is, but let's see if there is something there, okay?" I thought of last night's incident and Ted's story. "I have more to share, but I'd prefer to share it in person rather than over the phone."

"Sounds good. Are you able to meet for lunch today?"

"That works perfectly. Let's meet up at the Country Corner Café."

"And don't forget those documents! I can't wait to sink my teeth into them!" He chuckled.

The thought of potentially resolving whatever was going on with Ted and stopping the nightmares made my anxiety a whole lot better. I clutched my phone in my hands and let out a calming breath. We could fix this. After that, I could relax.

Arriving early at the café, I got Jacob and me a table. I asked for the curtains across my booth to be pulled down since the sun's orange gaze blinded my eyes. The restaurant always had that familiar smell of syrup mixed with sweet meats like bacon. My mouth watered as I anticipated the food. Southern food was always a comfort and reminded me of home, and their biscuits and gravy here were my favorite. I wished more restaurants here had fried steak and gravy or places with better fried chicken and creamed corn, but a girl sometimes had to make do with what she had.

Jacob entered through the doors of the café. Standing up, I hugged him before he took a seat across from me at the table. "How are you, Christina?" he asked.

I thought of Ted and how happy I was we were living together, but then that joy was quickly overshadowed by my worry about his mood swings and the experience I'd had last night. "I'm alright," I finally answered.

"That's good," he said.

The waitress came by, and we ordered coffee to start with.

"To be honest," I began. "I don't know if I'm allowed to have these papers and books."

Jacob smirked and rubbed his hands together. "I love it! It's like back in college when we stole those flyers around campus that were promoting an event hosted by our least favorite professor."

I laughed. "He was *so* mean!"

"He hated on my dyed 'fro."

Laughing so hard, I snorted. "Everyone hated on that. Toner colored hair went out of style in the '90s, kid. Nobody told you? Your hair looked like gold."

Jacob smiled. "Yeah, 'cause I was fly."

I rolled my eyes playfully. After looking over the menu and making our order, I took out my bag full of the documents from the house. I plopped down two heavy, leather-bound books, and a few papers came flying out onto the tiled floor. Jacob picked up the stray yellow pieces of aged paper and studied them. "How far back do these go?"

"To the early 1900s, I believe," I said as I put the last of the books onto the table.

Jacob rifled through one of the books, careful not to rip the fragile sheets as he sped through. "It appears to me these books are big notebooks filled with personal notes." He turned his attention to the stray pieces of paper and picked them up to read. "These lone papers are travel papers and…" He picked up another piece and furrowed his brow as he studied it, "and information about the house, like construction costs and all that." Stacking the four books on top of one another, he pushed them to the corner and focused on the stray papers instead. "I want to organize these in order of when they occurred. This way, I can follow a timeline." He paused. "What exactly am I looking for here?"

I opened my mouth as I thought of what to say. "The previous owner tried to kill Ted, and now he's having nightmares."

Jacob widened his eyes, and he opened his mouth to say something, but nothing came out.

"And I want to help him find closure, so I'm hoping these papers may help to find out if they belong to the previous owner in any way. If so, maybe we can help ease Ted's mind knowing there is nothing the previous owner can do…" I had to think of a lie and quick. "To possibly end his time early in prison."

"How old was his killer?" Jacob sounded like he was in disbelief. "These papers are so old."

I sighed and reached my hand out to grab Jacob's arm. "Please, just look through them for me. Please." I didn't want to explain what was truly going on because I feared Jacob would leave.

Jacob's eyes burrowed into mine as I pleaded silently. He slowly nodded. "Okay," he whispered with concern, "I'll help." He continued to scour over the documents when he leaned over the table and focused his attention on one document in particular. "This looks sketchy."

My heart leaped in my chest in both excitement and nervousness. "What is it?"

"The first owner of this land was a man named Charles Winterford. He owned the land itself originally. Not sure if the house was on the property yet or not, but there was an overlap of ownership between Winterford and a man named Dr. Ransteen." Jacob grabbed one of the thick books. He carefully opened it, but the cover seemed only to be held together by two thin strings, and it flopped onto the table. "These are some big notebooks."

"Maybe it was for documenting patients or budgeting. Dr. Ransteen ran a hospital on the property."

The waitress came by with our food and filled up our coffee cups. "Anything else I can get you?" she asked.

"No thanks, hon," I said with a smile.

Jacob was far too busy buried in one of the books to pay attention. "What is all this?" He closed up the book and then grabbed to open the second one, then the third, and finally the fourth. "These notebooks are filled with strange symbols and scribbles of notes in English." His eyes narrowed as he studied the books further. "I'm going to need more time to look over all of this, but this is an amazing find." He was silent as he continued to read over everything. I knew better than to disturb Jacob when he was in the zone. He always loved history, so his being a professor for the subject was a no-brainer. In his spare time, he worked on cold cases and even helped to reopen some cases. He was good, so I knew I could trust him to research anything about this house.

"I think…" Jacob paused as he read.

I leaned in.

"I think Dr. Ransteen was into some *dark* stuff." Jacob's tone sounded more enthralled than fearful. "I think he killed Waterford to take his land."

I perked up. "What? That's a fast assumption." My eyes widened as I tried to read over the book, but everything was a mess of scribbles: English mixed with strange symbols followed by Latin. Seeing it made me curl a bit inwards.

"Yeah, right here," said Jacob as he pointed at the notebook. "This book serves as a sort of diary of this guy, and he said he got 'rid' of the owner. I'm not sure what he meant by that, but the land was just gifted to Dr. Ransteen by Waterford after Waterford had put up some of his lands for sale. Why put it up for sale and then give it away for free to a total stranger?"

My knee shook, and I blinked several times. "Maybe we can look up who this Charles Waterford is and see if there is any further documentation of him."

"I'm sorry to cut our lunch short, but I want to get to the bottom of this. I'll have to take my food to-go. This is a great find, Christina," said Jacob.

His praise made me grimace.

The waitress came by and asked, "How are we doing here, folks?"

"We need a box," said Jacob.

"Make that two," I added.

Once the waitress was gone, Jacob turned his attention to me. "I love mysteries like these, and if Dr. Ransteen did kill Waterford, there is a murder he got away with. We'll figure this out. Give me more time. I know someone I can contact that can look into any information about Waterford. If there is any."

The waitress came by with a couple of to-go boxes, and we put our untouched food inside. Jacob put a piece of toast in his mouth. With the bread hanging out, he said, "I'll get back to you in a few days. Promise." He gathered up the books and papers in a rush and put his box of food on top of the stack. "This is good stuff. Good stuff," he said to himself as he left out the door.

Jacob always got real nerdy about things like this and seeing that excitement always made me giggle. Jacob rushed back into the café and said, "Oh! And bye, Christina. I'll talk to you soon!"

By the time I got home from our breakfast-for-lunch, Ted was sitting on the couch flipping through different Netflix titles.

"Hi, Teddy," I said. "How was work?"

Ted shrugged as he continued to search through different shows. "Same as always."

I grimaced. He no longer enjoyed his job or much of anything anymore. It was concerning. Walking over towards him, I ran my fingers through his hair. "Do ya want to go out today?"

Ted sat silently as he clicked the remote over and over.

I rubbed my hands up and down his back. "Teddy, hon. You should go out. Goin' straight to work and home isn't exactly the best." Ted shoved his shoulder away from me to show he wanted me to stop talking to him. I froze as my heart dropped to my stomach. Sighing, I walked away.

The rest of the day was spent mostly in silence. I busied myself with crocheting another scarf I'd probably give away as a gift for Christmas. Crocheting was relatively easy at this point, and I could finish a scarf in one day if I committed to it. Halfway through my project, I put it away into my crochet basket and looked over at Ted. He sat like a stoic robot on the couch. I decided to sit with him and attempt some cuddle time, but it was as if he was a zombie. While on the couch, I leaned over and kissed his cheek and then his nose. Instead of kissing me back or smiling like he used to, he stared blankly at the screen.

"Teddy," I said.

"Hm," he grunted.

Sucking in my lower lip, concern twisted at my chest. "What's going on in your head?"

He finally looked at me, but his eyes were glossed over. "Nothing."

I put my hand to his cheek, and my forehead creased. "Are you okay?"

Ted let out a huff before yanking his head out of my grasp. "I'm fine," he said through gritted teeth.

I dropped my hand. My heart sank low to my stomach once again.

He pinched the bridge of his nose and sighed. "Sorry. I'm just tired. I'm going to bed." He squeezed my hand softly before getting up and going to the bedroom.

Sighing, I sat back against the couch. I ran my hands down my face. At this point, he *had* to go on meds. This couldn't go on. Ted being in the bedroom told me he wanted to be alone, so I warmed up my food from the restaurant and ate the leftovers. Bundling up under my heavy-weight blanket, I watched some mindless feel-good shows. When things got too severe in any show, I'd get stressed out.

Shows without too big of a plot were a safe bet. Even romantic comedies made my stress levels soar.

When my eyelids got heavy, I turned off the television and debated whether or not I should go into the bedroom to sleep. My chest twisted at the thought of facing Ted's silent anger. Taking in a deep breath, I willed myself into the bedroom. I relaxed when I saw he was fast asleep.

That night, the shaking of the bed stirred me awake. Looking over my shoulder, I saw Ted kicking and flailing his arms against the mattress. I put my hands onto his arm. "Teddy," I said. "Wake up. Ted." He didn't wake up, but the moving suddenly stopped.

I laid back down and tried to fall back asleep. Right as I was deep enough asleep, the bed began to shake again from Ted's jolting.

I got up out of bed and grabbed my pillow before huffling over to the couch to plop down. I sighed as I stared up at the ceiling. My eyelids were heavy as I yawned. Our mattress squeaked and rustled as Ted continued to shake, punch, and kick in his sleep. Getting any sleep in that room was futile at this point. Good thing it was the weekend for me because I don't think I would've had the energy for work. It was already two in the morning by the time I finally was able to fall back asleep in the living room.

The smell of coffee woke me up in the morning. The orange light from the morning sun shined through our purple curtains by the front door, blanketing over me on the couch. Ted sat at the kitchen table, sipping on his coffee as he scrolled through his phone. "Hey, Teddy," I said as I yawned.

He looked up at me. "Good morning," he said in a kind tone. "I have coffee made."

I studied his face to judge how he felt today. He seemed to be more alive this morning, and more cheerful, which relaxed my anxiety.

"Going to bed early last night was a good idea. I feel great," he said. He grinned.

I gave a soft smile. "Good." I got up and groaned as my heavy eyes struggled to stay open. Trudging over to the kitchen table, I sat down holding the fresh cup of coffee Ted got for me. "You were kicking and punching in your sleep again."

His smile diminished a bit. "I'm sorry that you had to move to the couch. It's been a while since you had to do that."

I smiled real big to show it was okay because I didn't want him to feel bad. "I know, hon." I yawned. "I'm so happy I have no work today."

"You're lucky," he said with a smile. "Maybe I can take work off so we can spend the day together or something."

I perked up a bit. My heart fluttered. "Really?" I was delighted he wanted to do something. That meant he was doing better mentally today.

He shrugged. "Sure! Why not?"

"Thanks, hon," I said taking a sip of my coffee.

He leaned over the table and gave me a small peck on the lips.

"I'm glad you are doing so well today," I said. "I was a bit worried."

"I know, and I'm sorry about my mood lately." He grabbed ahold of my hand. His lips fit into a tight line. "I'm sorry that you had to move to the couch. It's been a while since you've had to do that again."

I smiled to show him I wasn't bothered by it. "I know, hon."

"It's strange, though, because, for me, I had a good night's rest." He chuckled as he shook his head. "Odd."

Kissing his cheek, I said, "Maybe you were working through something and got through it."

Ted let out a sigh. "Yeah…" He went quiet, and the strained look in his eyes told me he was holding something back.

Worry seeped into my heart, causing my chest to constrict as always. "What is it?"

Ted was silent, but after a moment, he shook his head. "Nothing." He plastered on a smile. "Nothing, I promise."

I eyed him warily, but I decided to let it go just this once. Usually, I pried to appease my anxiety, but I didn't want to make his good day turn bad, not with Ted's recent mood swings.

Ted opened his phone and looked at the time. "I should get going. I'll ask if I can get off early today," he said.

I leaned over and kissed him. He kissed me back softly. "Okay, hon." I rested my head on his shoulder for a minute, soaking in this rare, peaceful moment before he had to leave for work.

After he left, I continued to sip my coffee as I sat in our quiet apartment. My heavy eyelids told me to ditch the coffee and head back to bed. The sound of my cell phone going off stirred me awake. Fumbling with my blanket, I managed to dig my head and arms out. I rolled over towards the nightstand and blinked a few times before grabbing my phone.

It was Jacob.

My adrenaline shot through my body, waking me up entirely. Maybe he finally found something we could use to help us. Quickly, I pressed to accept the call. "Jacob! What do you got for me?"

Jacob sighed before laughing. "I cannot believe the case you gave me."

I couldn't help but smile. "Yeah? Is it everything you'd hoped it'd be?"

"This is probably one of the best cold cases I have ever worked on. I dug up some history on this house, and it seems the original owner, Charles Waterford, disappeared after he had contact with Dr. Ransteen. Why nobody suspected foul play, I have no clue. They ended up finding his body years later, and the only reason why they knew it was Waterford was because his engraved pocket watch was found with his remains."

I sat up. "Are you serious?"

"Yes! I don't know how to prove it was Dr. Ransteen, but here's another spin to the story. Remember how I said the doctor was involved in some dark stuff?"

I yawned. "Yes."

"I went through his notebooks and travel papers, and I found some letters between him and someone named H.H. In one of the letters, both Ransteen and this mystery person planned to meet in Chicago where this person lived. I think it might have been H.H. Holmes."

My forehead creased in confusion. "What? Like the serial killer H.H. Holmes?"

"Yes! H.H. mentioned he was a doctor, and Ransteen was interested in his work. Ransteen traveled to Chicago to visit him, and that's where H.H. Holmes lived."

I raised my eyebrows in surprise and was somewhat dismayed. "Wow. That's crazy if it's true, but there's no guarantee it's the infamous serial killer."

"Think of it this way: what are the chances of there being another doctor in Chicago around that time that also went by the name H.H. and who also had a sketchy past?"

I swayed my head side to side as I took in the theory. "It is very coincidental." I ran my fingers through my hair, and they got stuck in the knots. After yanking my fingers free, I said, "but this is strange and interesting at the same time. Thanks for letting me know what you have so far."

"No problem. There's still more I want to research here. When I learn more, I'll give you a call. Perhaps we should meet up with Ted, and we can really dive into this."

I blinked several times. Ted would not like that. In fact, he'd be upset I reached out to Jacob in the first place. "Um… We'll see."

"Okay. Well, let's have brunch again soon anyway. Take care."

My arms fell limp at my side after I hung up. I swallowed hard after a moment when the realization hit me of what this meant: Ted was in danger.

Chapter Three
Ted's Rage

The dark shadow continued its pursuit after me as I tried to escape its clutches down the cemented hallway. I had no idea where I was, but I knew I had to get out—my heart was beating ferociously against my chest, threatening to break free. My lungs weakened, and my legs were ready to give out. The hallway kept going on endlessly. There seemed to be a light source coming from nowhere. The back of my neck developed a cold sweat as the black cloud inched its way closer. A person began to take form further down the cemented hallway, but no matter how hard I ran, I could never seem to reach him or her.

"Teddy, hon," I heard Christina's voice call out.

Where was she? My eyes darted around, but there was only cement. I called out her name, "Christina! Where are you?" Whomever this person was at the end of the hallway reached out their hand, but I was not close enough to grab it.

I heard Christina scream and yell, "Ted! Wake up!"

I lost my footing as my body convulsed.

"You need to get up!" yelled the mysterious person. It was a man's voice.

The cloud enveloped me. I couldn't breathe. It was so cold. I opened my mouth to take in a deep gulp of air.

"Don't!" yelled the man. He was now close enough I could make out some of his features. He wore brown slacks with suspenders over a loose, white T-shirt. I know I knew him from somewhere, but I couldn't figure out where.

With my mouth now open, desperate for air, the black swarm invaded my mouth and ran down my throat, sending a jolt through me.

"Ted!" I heard Christina yell.

Finally, I blinked awake and saw Christina's wide-eyed stare. She was visibly shaking, and I immediately sat up and grabbed her hand as fear shot through me like a knife slicing into my stomach. "What's wrong? What happened?" I asked. "You look so scared." I stroked the side of her face to calm her. I didn't like it when she worried too much because she was already so anxious all the time as it was. She blinked, and some of the fear seemed to melt away.

"Th-There was…" She took a deep, short breath in and out. "I heard scratchin'… I heard… a-a growl."

The immense terror in her eyes made me grab her and hold her close to me. I wanted to take it all away. This should be happening only to *me*. Not her.

The nightmares were becoming more violent. This wasn't good, and I still felt that clammy dampness inside me left behind from the black cloud. I shivered. I needed to shake it off.

We didn't sleep for the rest of that night, but I was used to it; Christina wasn't. I held her hand as I watched her stare up at the ceiling. Her eyes darted back and forth, and she flinched at any little sound. Swallowing hard, I knew I had to do something. I couldn't let this happen to her too.

When the sun finally rose, I got myself up to take a shower. Work would be rough, but one of us had to go so the bills could be paid. Since I was used to the nightmares at this point, it was only fair I go to work so Christina could rest. I got out of the shower and dried myself off. Facing my reflection in the mirror, I noticed new wrinkles forming on my face. Nobody told me your thirties would be *this* rough.

I went into our bedroom to get dressed and saw the bags under Christina's eyes. "Stay home today," I told to her as I grabbed my scrubs out of the closet. "You need it."

Christina rested her head in her hand. "I can tough it out."

After dressing myself, I walked over to her and kissed her forehead. "You shouldn't have to. Stay home. I got this today." I caressed her cheek, which made her smile softly.

She didn't put up much of a fight, which told me she had to be beyond exhausted. "Okay," she said as she plopped back onto her pillow.

At work, I spent the day as usual, but I found I didn't have the energy to go the extra mile. There was this foreign feeling of ice that swept through me at all times, causing my blood to run cold. I attempted to ignore it as I pressed on with my shift. I went to Mr. Foster's room to give him his medicine along with some juice. Mr. Foster sat up in his bed expectantly, and he searched my hands with his eyes before they fell flat with disappointment.

"What's wrong?" I asked. "Not the right meds?"

He sat back against the pillows. "No. Nothing."

I placed the pills in one hand and the juice in the other. I put my hands in the pockets of my scrubs. "Anything else I can do for you?" I asked.

Mr. Foster looked at his pills in his hands and then up at me. The emotion in his eyes was unfamiliar to me. Sadness? Concern? "No. No. Thank you."

I nodded my head. "Okay. I will see you again soon when it's time for lunch." Heading out the door to the other line of patients waiting for me in their rooms, I sighed before I entered through each door. Around lunchtime, I went into the cafeteria and saw the basket of peaches and apples. Realization dawned on me. That's what Mr. Foster must've been upset about earlier: I didn't bring him his usual gift in the morning.

I reached over to grab the peach and ground my teeth together. It was unlike me to miss something like this, but then again, I didn't have the same drive as before to keep going above and beyond what I was paid to do. The heavy weight of disappointment made it hard to breathe.

Ben came by and slapped his hand on my back. "What's up!"

It shocked the feeling of distress away. His loud and booming voice made me flinch, which I was used to, but for some reason, today it made me irritated. Instead of risking a fight with him, I gripped tightly to Mr. Foster's food tray and huffed out a short "Hi" before I stomped away from Ben. I didn't want to do something I'd regret, so it was best I got out of there. By the time I turned the corner, I had let out a breath that relieved me. I didn't lash out at him. I was able to get away in time, but why was I so easily upset today? And out of nowhere? That's when I remembered I had an appointment with a psychiatrist that day. Maybe I needed the meds. Maybe Carlos and Christina were right.

Clocking out of work was like a breath of fresh air. This heaviness I didn't even realize was there was lifted once I punched out. I got into my old pickup truck and sat there for a moment. Resting my head on the steering wheel, attempting to relax, I still felt that damp cold inside me. I had no idea where it was coming from. Turning on the heater in my truck, I hoped it'd help. As my truck warmed up, I checked the local news on my phone.

The top headline stated: Infamous Saratoga House Demolishment Goes Awry.

My heart sank, and I clicked to read the article. It said they had completed the demolishment, but something went wrong with the house's basement part. Despite following the typical protocol, the destruction of the home caused a sinkhole on the property.

I was a little shocked. Perhaps the house had a life of its own and didn't want to get demolished. With my car sufficiently warmed up, I put it in drive and headed to my appointment.

The psychiatrist was located at the local hospital in a separate wing from the emergency area. Parking outside the facility, I stared at the bay windows that lined the outside. There were benches and a lot of shrubbery and roses planted along the building. I suppose that was their way of making the place seem warm and inviting.

I got out of the truck and chewed on the inside of my cheek as I debated ditching my appointment altogether. What got my feet moving towards the entrance was the thought of

Christina and how my mood swings must have been affecting her.

This was for her. Not me.

At least that's what I told myself as I went inside and checked in for my appointment. Turning to face the waiting room, I saw people of various ages staring at their phones or reading a newspaper. I took a seat in the corner of the waiting room far away from everyone else. Part of me just wanted to crawl into a hole and stay there. I wrapped my jacket tightly around me and rested my shoulder against the wall.

After several minutes, a nurse came out, calling my name. I followed her through the door. "Dr. Lockhart will be with you shortly," said the nurse. "Take a seat here." She gestured to enter a room. There was a desk beside a window with a computer on it. On the other side of the room was a couch, coffee table, and a couple of armchairs. The lights were off, but the large window provided ample lighting. I gingerly took a seat on the couch, and my knee shook as I waited for the doctor. Eyeing the coffee table, there was a shallow dish full of hard candies. On a corner table beside the couch was a lamp and a bowl of knick-knacks like stress balls, miniature Rubik's Cubes, and other fidget toys.

After several minutes, the doctor came in. It was a woman in her mid-forties who wore a long, white lab coat over her pencil skirt and peach blouse. Her blonde hair was pulled back into a ponytail, and her bright blue eyes sparkled as she smiled a greeting at me. "How are we doing today, Ted?" she asked. She reached her hand over and shook mine. Her handshake was sturdy and robust. "My name is Dr. Lockhart."

She took a seat at the armchair across from me and crossed her long legs. "Dr. Whitaker reached out to me; I understand you are not exactly keen on seeing a psychiatrist. I don't blame you," she laughed lightly. "Many people don't want to be put on medication because of the stigma. I know I felt the same way when I was a young woman struggling."

I furrowed my brow a little. "You take medication too?"

She leaned back into the armchair. "Oh, yes! I struggled with chronic depression, and I didn't even know it until I experienced life without it. I thought, 'I'm not crazy. I don't see things. I don't need it. I know I'm just not doing well right now.'"

She hit the nail on the head, to which I nodded my head.

She smiled pleasantly. "What I didn't understand was how much I wasn't functioning. I was barely keeping my head above water. I was surviving, but just barely. I had no idea that not wanting to kill yourself wasn't the only goal here. I lacked ambition, motivation, a lust for life, and so on." She let out a laugh. "My room was a constant mess; my motivation was so bad."

I chuckled, which made me relax my posture a bit.

"You should have seen it. Stacks of crap I couldn't bring myself to get rid of because I had no drive. I'd buy new clothes just to avoid the laundry."

I smirked. "I'm pretty sure that's just laziness."

She shrugged. "Perhaps, but now my home is spotless because I gained back my drive. My drive to do things like taking care of myself, to find hobbies, and to live a successful life." She used air quotes. "'Laziness' can sometimes be a symptom, but we call it lack of motivation."

It was silent for a moment. The silence made me pick at my jeans. She eyed my mannerisms, which made me more nervous.

"So tell me what has been going on," she said.

I swallowed.

She leaned in a little. "I'm not here to tick off boxes to see if you need to be forced to take medication. The choice is ultimately yours. There is zero pressure here. I just want to share another healing option to aid you through this time." She grinned. "You can either take it or leave it."

Her saying that helped to alleviate the pressure, which made me want to open up more. "I had moved into a house a few years ago in the hopes of helping my mother, and…" I trailed off as I thought of that night in the basement. Biting down hard, I hadn't noticed my body had tensed until Dr. Lockhart said, "Relax. It's okay."

I forced my posture to relax, but it left me feeling shaky. "Ever since that night, I have been having nightmares about it. I get agitated easily over stupid things that wouldn't normally upset me. I was never an angry person." My memory flashed of my fights with my father when my mother was still alive and my frustration with him over how he was caring for her. "Well, unless provoked."

Dr. Lockhart nodded.

"And it's affecting my relationship with my friends and family now."

"When did your mother pass away, if you don't mind my asking?"

"About two years ago," I said.

"Is that when the agitation started?"

Shaking my head, I said, "No, it started before that, even while my mother was alive, because of her illness. I wanted to help, and I thought I could…" I looked away and sighed. "I thought I could fix her somehow."

She nodded. "You wanted control of the situation, which is normal because you felt so out of control. The fact is you couldn't help her. You couldn't stop the boulder from rolling down the hill, but you wanted to."

I chewed on my lip, feeling frustrated. A painful mixture of grief and anger weighed on my chest. I wanted to stop talking about this.

"You were grieving even before her death, and you still are after the fact. That's a normal response. On top of grief, you are healing from a traumatic experience you faced alongside your mother, which amplifies the state you're in now." Her small smile forced me to relax a little. "The way you're responding to all this is completely okay and normal. Anyone would be this way, so stop beating yourself up. Allow yourself to feel."

I stared down at my hands, which continued to fidget with a loose string in my jeans. Her words brought a wave of relief. Being told I was allowed to feel human was freeing.

"I want to try medication with you, but you do not have to take it if you don't want to. I think it'll help with your sleep and anxiety, which I think is what is contributing to the irritability."

Annoyance built up in my chest; I sighed to release it. "I don't have to take it?"

She shook her head with a smile. "No. It is your body, your choice." She went to her desk and opened her drawer to take out a small prescription notepad and pen. "I will prescribe you some medication, and if you don't want to take it, don't. You don't even have to pick it up from the pharmacy if you don't want to. It's totally up to you." She hurried over to me in her high heels. "No pressure."

Staring blankly at the paper, I finally took it. I managed a grimace. "Thanks."

"You're welcome." She took a seat behind her desk. "That concludes our session today. I'd like to reschedule for a month from now, if that's okay with you."

I ran my fingers through my hair. "Yeah, sure."

Once I left the doctor's office, I sat in my truck staring at the prescription note, feeling the same way I did about showing my terrible report card to my parents back in high school. The pressure weighed heavily on me was lessened because I didn't technically have to do anything if I didn't want to. I kept telling myself that over and over as I shoved the note into my glove compartment and drove home.

Christina wasn't home when I arrived. Figuring she went out for lunch again or something, I plopped onto the couch. I ripped off my nametag and tossed it across the sofa. Sitting there silently was too much for me. I was afraid of where my mind would wander.

My mother.

The house.

Dr. Ransteen.

I sat up and shook off the chill that trod down my spine like a sinister snake. Hoping to ease the agitation that began to build up, I bit down on my teeth. The television seemed inviting, so I turned it on and began flipping through the channels. Nothing seemed appetizing to watch, but the act of pushing a button over and over distracting my mind with random images from the screen was enough to soothe me; however, only a little.

A few minutes later, Christina came through the door. She paused there for a moment. I could hear her keys jingle as she nervously played with her fingers. From the corner of my eye, I could see her studying me.

"Hi, Teddy," she said in her usual cheerful tone. I sneered at the fact that it sounded extra joyful, as if she was compensating for my sour mood. It annoyed me. "How was work?"

I shrugged. She was only asking a simple question, but for some reason, my anger boiled. The snake was back in my spine again, and I could feel its tongue poking at the fire in my chest, making it grow. I found my thoughts becoming more irritated.

What the hell did Christina mean by "how was work"? She knows how it went. It was boring and not fulfilling at all.

"Same as always," I managed to say. Continuously clicking through channels helped to channel some of the unnecessary anger a bit.

She came towards me and ran her fingers through my hair, which was somewhat soothing, but there was this dark pit in my core that wanted to reject it. "Do ya want to go out today?"

Rather than answer her and risk snapping, I kept flipping through the channels.

Her touch on my back made the dampness from the snake inch itself closer around my heart. It made the heavy air around me become unstable. Christina spoke, but I didn't hear her words. I just wanted the touching to stop, so I shoved my shoulder away from her.

I should just go to bed. Stop being such a nuisance to Christina.

I got up and left for the bedroom. It was as if right when I closed the door my mind went blank. Before I knew it, I was up and awake in my bedroom. I furrowed my brow as I sat up, surveying my surroundings. How did I get to the bed? I had *just* closed the door when…

The sun shined through our window. Its bright yellow color told me it had to be before noon. I shook my head as I tried to make sense of the time gap. Was I dreaming the whole time, and I now just woke up? Or did I not remember my evening at all from yesterday? Both answers equally terrified me.

I *had* to have dreamed about an entire day because later on in the dream there was the strangest moment of me watching myself on the couch with Christina. She was trying to cuddle me and talk to me, but I kept dismissing her before leaving. It was as if I had no control over my body. I shook my head, wanting to get a grip on myself.

I'm just tired is all.

I patted the side of me where Christina typically slept, but she wasn't there. Maybe she woke up before me. When I went out to the living room, I saw she was passed out on the couch. Sighing heavily, I knew I must've been tossing and turning in my sleep again. Clicking my tongue in disappointment at myself, I decided to make some coffee.

The fresh smell of the beans comforted me a bit. After I had made my cup and took a few sips, Christina stirred awake. "Hey, Teddy," she said with a yawn.

Her usual bed head made me smirk. A warmth overtook me at that moment as I gazed at her. I loved her so damn much it ached sometimes. It was a strange feeling, but one I gladly embraced. "Good morning," I said. "I have coffee made."

Usually, I woke up beyond exhausted as if I'd gotten no sleep at all, but this morning, I felt rejuvenated and refreshed. I felt like a new man. Maybe I was in some deep sleep and fabricated a whole day in a dream.

Christina came to the table to drink her coffee with me. "You were kicking and punching in your sleep again."

I almost forgot about the memory lapse. My smile faltered. "I'm sorry that you had to move to the couch," I said. "It's been a while since you had to do that."

She smiled that usual grin that told me she didn't want me to feel bad. "I know, hon." She yawned. "I'm so happy I have no work today."

"You're lucky," I said with a smile. "Maybe I can take work off so we can spend the day together or something."

She perked up, and seeing her joy in that statement filled my heart with warmth. "Really?"

I shrugged. "Sure! Why not?" Besides, my morning was doing great so far. I didn't want to ruin it with going to a job I didn't exactly enjoy so much anymore.

"Thanks, hon," she said, taking a sip of her coffee.

I leaned over the table and gave her a small peck on the lips.

"I'm glad you are doing so well today," she said. "I was a bit worried."

"I know, and I'm sorry about my mood lately." I reached over to hold her. My lips fit into a tight line. "I'm sorry that you had to move to the couch. It's been a while since you've had to do that again."

She smiled, which I knew that smile. It was a smile to show me she was okay and to not feel guilty. "I know, hon."

"It's strange, though, because, for me, I had a good night's rest." I managed a chuckle, but then I thought of my dream. I was dreaming of watching *me*. Was that real? Did that really happen, and I didn't know it? "Odd," I added.

"Maybe you were working through something and got through it."

I knew that was a lie, but I didn't want Christina to worry any more than she already has been. She tended to be a worrywart. I let out a sigh. "Yeah…" I stared blankly at my coffee cup, trying to remember if that dream was real or not.

"What is it?"

I blinked. "Nothing." Shaking my head, I forced a smile across my face. "Nothing, I promise." Having work to get to, I kissed Christina goodbye and went on my way.

Work was a lot easier today. I had more pep in my walk, and I ignored the lack of remembrance of last night. Today I remembered to grab that peach for Mr. Foster. "Quick, catch!" I said as I lightly tossed it over to him.

His smile brightened my day even more. "Thanks. I see you're feeling better."

"Oh, you bet," I said as I turned on my heel. "Need anything else?"

He waved me off with his wrinkled and nimble hand. "No, no. You go take care of the old people. Leave us young ones alone," he winked.

I lightly chuckled. "Okay, Mr. Foster."

Ben walked by me in the hallway, and he held his head down. I frowned, knowing our growing rift was my fault, and today I wanted to mend that more than anything. "Hey," I said. Ben looked up, almost surprised I spoke to him. "How have you been?" I asked.

Ben paused, almost confused. "Uh… Okay, sometimes."

I rubbed the back of my head. "Listen, I'm sorry about how I've been lately. I've just been…" I paused as I tried to find the words to explain best the fact I was having nightmares and Christina was now hearing ghosts too. "Going through a lot."

Ben stood up straight as he surveyed me. "Yeah, I know, bud."

Knowing Ben was going through grief too, but without all the added anger issues, made me feel more like crap. I looked down at the ground, and my cheeks warmed from embarrassment. "There's no excuse, but I'm trying."

Ben nodded his head. "Yeah, I get it." He gave me a small smirk, which was when I knew he had forgiven me.

"Want to go out for drinks with me after work today?" I asked.

Ben's eyes widened, and he perked up. "Sure, man! I'm down!"

"Alright, we'll meet at our usual spot then around six. What time do you get off?"

"Seven," said Ben with a sigh. "It's a long shift. I've been picking up extra hours."

"I get it. Let's meet there tonight."

The Parting Glass was our favorite bar in town, and it had been months since I last went there. On top of wanting to stay away from alcohol altogether out of fear I'd end up hooked to it like my father now was, I didn't have the motivation to be around my friends or other people. For once, I finally had the energy to. For the first time in a long time, I was having a good day. By the end of my shift, I even convinced myself all of it wasn't real, and I was just so tired that I had a peculiarly vivid dream.

I called Christina after work and told her, "I'm heading off to the bar with Ben."

Christina's voice was overjoyed, "Okay! Have fun, hon."

The sun was setting by the time I arrived, and since it was the middle of the work week, the place wasn't too packed. The smell of peanuts mixed with freshly cooked French fries filled my nostrils. A feel of comfort took over me as I stepped in and took a seat at the bar. The counter was made of wood, and it wrapped around from one side of the wall to the other. The tables had green checkered cloths on top of them, and there were dartboards at one end of the bar. Everything was as I remembered it, with the wood walls and green-colored flooring.

I ordered myself a beer and some fries to snack on. Ben came in several minutes later, throwing open the door and waving at me by flailing his arms around. Ben was a hyperactive fellow, but he meant well. He took a seat next to me at the bar and ordered himself an IPA. "So how was work, man?" he asked.

I shrugged. "It's not as fulfilling as it once was," I finally admitted.

Ben grimaced. "I've noticed."

I took a swig of my beer.

"I mean, it's hard not to notice that sour puss face all day." He put his hand on my shoulder and shook it. "We've all been worried."

"I know. It's been rough lately." I sighed before smiling to show I was now okay. "It's been rough for you too."

Ben's eyes squinted in pain before he looked away. He downed nearly half his beer before shaking his head. "No. Um…" He paused. "Just… Not right now."

Nodding, I understood in that moment to not bring up Monica.

"I get it," said Ben. "You don't have to say it. I know what happened, and then with your mom passing…" he trailed off. "We get it that you needed time. How is your dad?" Ben got a new drink and took a sip.

Stress formed in my stomach, causing it to twist in knots. The truth was I hadn't spoken to my father in months. The last time we spoke was last Thanksgiving, and he had laid heavily into the drinking before then shortly after my mother's passing. He moved out of the cabin they had up in the mountains because it reminded him too much of her, and he moved in with my sister in New York City, where there were plenty more bars to choose from. "I haven't spoken to him. Not since our fight," I finally said.

Ben clicked his tongue. "That's a shame. What exactly happened, if you don't mind me asking?"

I sighed and took a chug of my beer. "You know how our relationship was even before my mother…" I trailed off.

"We never fully got along, and his idea of parenting was about teaching me to be a man."

"Which probably meant lots of abuse," added Ben. "Yeah, my father was the same damn way. He died years ago, though."

I smirked. Ben and I first bonded over the fact we shared the same strained relationships with our fathers, which was such a cliché: their fathers' disappointing sons who only ever wanted their praise. It was a tale as old as time. "My comfort was taken away, you know, when my mother died. She was my go-to on everything, and with that gone, I realized she was the only thing threading me to my father." I chugged some more before wiping my mouth to continue. "With her gone, that rift just grew. And his drinking problem made everything worse. He hit my sister one night after a forced dinner she tried to piece together for Thanksgiving."

Ben's eyes widened. "What? Are you serious?"

I took another big gulp of my beer, hoping it'd wash away the grief that began to bubble to the surface. "I stepped in and lost my temper, and my father and I brawled it out before I stormed out."

"Damn." Ben took a sip of his beer. "That's some shit, man. How is your sister doing about all of that?"

I shrugged. "She tries to call me, but I blame myself for the altercation becoming too violent. It's easier to ignore it, which I know is wrong. I just can't bring myself to face her."

Ben blew out some air and whistled. "I'm sorry. That sucks."

Getting that entire mess off my chest was uplifting. It made the heavy cloud that was always pulling me down a little lighter, and I felt I could breathe better. Ben and I laughed about the old times and continued drinking beer after beer. Before we knew it, it was late in the evening, and we were far too intoxicated to drive ourselves home.

I picked up my cell. The apps spun in circles, and it took far too long to dial Christina's number. When she picked up, I managed to slur out, "Hey there, pretty lady."

Christina giggled. "Yes, Teddy?"

"Ben and I…" I pointed at Ben, and he pointed at me. "We both need rides, my beautiful love."

Christina continued to giggle. "I'm glad y'all had fun. Tell the bartender to keep y'all out of trouble until I get there."

"Noooo promises!" Then I hung up. I pointed at the bartender. "Hey, my girl said you have to babysit us until she gets here." I threw down a twenty-dollar tip.
The man behind the counter laughed. "Sure thing. Want some water? More fries?"

"A burger, please!"

"Make it two!" added Ben.

Though we knew full well we were acting like fools, Ben and I had a good time. It was nice to let loose and laugh finally. The laughing felt great and so releasing, as if with each smile a little bit of darkness was removed from within me.

In the car with Christina and Ben, Ben poked at my shoulder. "Hey, I gotta tell you some shit."

"What's that?" My eyes were barely open at this point.

"Monica."

If I weren't so drunk, I knew the mention of Monica would have made me on edge. I noticed Christina eyeing Ben. "Yeah?" I said questioningly.

"She was into some weird shit, man. I think…" He blew out a breath. "I think whatever she was into is what got her killed."

This made me sit up. I let out a breath to calm myself.

Ben whirled his head around. "Her death really beat me up, you know? We were dating when she was murdered by that fucker."

"I know…" I went quiet.

"The last thing she said to me was 'follow the astral realm.' Like, what is that?"

I looked to Christina whose eyes were wide in what I thought to be intrigue.

"What is the astral realm?"

Ben ran his fingers through his hair. "The hell if I know. She left me all these books and notes of hers, and I've been sitting on them for a while. I figured it was some weird pagan religion she was into, and I put them in storage." Ben went quiet. His eyes dropped close.

I needed to know more. I shook his shoulder, making his head bob back and forth.

"Huh?" he said startled.

"Did she tell you anything else?" I asked.

"No, but I know you two were close. I always thought you knew something, but then your mother died, and you completely shut down. I've been keeping it in for all these years." His face pinched up. "It's painful, man. I think

I loved her." His eyes dropped down, but not from drunkendness. "I *know* I loved her."

I could tell tears were about to fall. I playfully punched his arm. "I know. I know."

He sniffed and blinked. "She was quirky as all hell, but I liked it, and I figured she was a little messed up since her sister, Lavinia, was killed. The weird thing is I think Monica knew she was going to die because the day before she disappeared she just dropped off a bunch of stuff and said to give it to you when the time was right. Then she said that thing about astral realm."

Christina and I eyed one another. "Ben," I said.

His eyes were closing.

"Ben!"

His eyes shot awake. "Huh?"

"Call me about this tomorrow, okay?"

"'Kay 'kay."

"Are you gonna remember?"

It was too late; Ben was passed out next to me in the back seat by the time we pulled up to Ben's apartment. Christina reached over and slapped Ben awake and said, "Get on inside."

Ben patted my shoulder as a goodbye and sauntered out of the car. Seeing Ben trip over his own shoes made me chuckle.

"I'm glad ya had fun," said Christina as we drove home.

Rubbing my face, I tried to catch my bearings. My body ached for some water and more food. "Yeah. It was just what I needed. We drank a little too much." I burped. "I never knew Ben was holding onto all that." I let out a sigh. "I wonder if he'll be okay."

"I think he will," said Christina. "Reach out to him tomorrow." She patted my knee. "But I'm glad you had some fun tonight. You really needed it." It was quiet for a moment as we continued our drive back to our home. Christina looked at me briefly before turning her eyes back to the road. "I'm glad you had a good day today, hon. I've been worried."

I laid my head back against the seat. "I know. I was too. Hopefully this mood keeps."

Christina smiled. "I think it will. How was the psychiatrist today?"

I nearly rolled my eyes at the thought of taking medicine. "It was okay. I'm still debating whether or not to do the medicine route."

"Well, it'll only help," she said.

Once we arrived home, Christina held my hand as we walked into the apartment. "Go lay down, hon," she said. "I'll get ya dinner ready to fill up that stomach of yours."

Filling up a cup of water, I left to nap off the strong buzz before the food was ready. After dinner, with a slight hangover forming by the end of the night, I held Christina in my arms as we watched television. I was more relaxed than I had been in months.

When it was time for bed that night, I dreamt of blackness. There was no ground. No air. No walls. Just a black abyss and I tried to claw my way out. As I got further into the blackness, an overwhelming sense of panic constricted my chest. Adrenaline shot through me, and I continued to swim through the abyss to find an exit. I tried to call out, but it was as if the environment prevented it. That was when the air became thicker like jelly, and I couldn't breathe. It became harder to swim through the blackness.

"Follow the astral realm," said a woman's voice. Was that Monica?

I tried to find where it was coming from, but it echoed all around me.

"The answer is in the fold," said the woman.

I told myself, 'You are dreaming. Wake up. Wake up!'

"Ted?" I heard Christina's voice echo. It was distorted, and I couldn't make out where it was coming from.

"Christina!" I screamed in my head.

"Ted, what are ya doin'?" her voice said.

I frantically tried to escape, but with no clear path, I was lost. I forced my eyes closed, and when I opened them, I was standing in the kitchen. Furrowing my brow, I looked down at my hands, then my feet. To make sure it was all realm I pinched myself. I glanced through the window at the quarter moon that shined in the night sky.

"Teddy?" I heard Christina's voice.

I turned around.

She was standing by our bedroom door. "What are ya doin' up?"

Glancing around, I was unable to find my words. "I…" I looked down at my feet again. "I was dreaming." The unsettling fear and concern that swam through my body was enough to make me want to cry. My knees shook a little.

Christina blinked before making her way over to me. "Hon, this happens sometimes. My brother used to sleepwalk during his night terrors. Were you havin' a nightmare?" She held my face in her hands, which soothed me.

I nodded.

Christina kissed my cheek. "Come on, hon. Let's go to bed. It's okay."

I stared back at where I stood in the kitchen as I made my way back to bed, completely dismayed. Falling asleep was not going to happen, so I stayed up watching YouTube videos on my phone with headphones in.

When Christina woke up in the morning, I felt safe falling asleep, knowing she could wake me up if I climbed out of bed unknowingly. I didn't have work since it was my weekend, so it wasn't a problem for me to sleep in until the late afternoon.

When I finally woke up again, I heard Christina's voice beyond the bedroom door. Then I heard an unknown male voice mumbling alongside hers. I pulled the covers off me, curious as to who was here. Maybe it was Ben coming over to nurse his hangover with us. My head swam and beat sharply, which made me wince. Opening the bedroom door, I saw a man sitting at our kitchen table with Christina. Spread across the table were the leather-bound books and aged papers Christina had taken from the old house.

"What's going on?' I asked as I rubbed my head.

Christina looked up at me and jumped out of her seat to grab me a cup of coffee. She raced over to me with some medicine in her palm. "Here, take this for the headache I'm sure ya must have right about now. This is Jacob." She pointed at the man at the table. He had a goatee and curly black hair that was cut close to his head. He stood up, and he towered over me as he shook my hand.

82

"It's nice to meet you, Ted. Christina has told me all about you," he said with a perfect smile.

I stared him up and down. "Sure." My mood today was not the same as yesterday. Maybe it was because of the dream or the sleepwalking or perhaps the hangover, but I didn't like that Jacob was here.

Jacob was taller, and judging by his arms, he was stronger too. A hot spit formed in my mouth from this emotion I wasn't familiar with. Jealousy? I was not too fond of Christina being alone with any guy. When he left back to the table, I pulled Christina aside. "Who is this guy?" I said through gritted teeth.

Christina pulled her arm out of my grasp. "He's my friend from back home. He moved here not too long ago. He's here to help."

That seemed to make me more upset he knew her longer than I did. I peered over at the table and glowered. "Help with what?"

Christina furrowed her brow. "What's wrong with you?"

"I don't want some strange guy in *my* home talking to you like that."

"Like what?" Christina put her hand on her hip and raised an eyebrow. "I can talk to whomever, whenever. You're just jealous."

I ground my teeth together. My unfounded rage took the front seat, but the other part of me—the *real* me—couldn't understand why I was so upset. It was as if I had no control over my feelings. Why was I so enraged?

"This isn't like you," said Christina as she took a step away from me.

"Yeah, because this fucking guy is here. What the fuck do you think?"

Woah...

That wasn't like me. I instantly regretted my words, but it was like they spilled out like word vomit.

Christina's lips got tiny and wrinkled. They did that when she was furious. She pointed to the door. "Get out."

Right then, it was like a switch flipped, and my anger ceased to exist. I stood there for a moment, completely dumbfounded at the quick change in mood. "I—" I stammered.

"Out!" she yelled.

Blinking, I grabbed my shoes and jacket and headed out the door. I noticed Jacob
eyeing me as if studying me before I shut the door behind me. Leaning against the door, I let out a huge breath. I would never dream of cussing at Christina, but there I was doing it. My sour mood was worse today than it ever has been. Disappointed in myself, I lightly knocked my head against the door. What the hell was happening to me?

Chapter Four

Christina Connects the Dots

"Get out!" I yelled. I saw literal red at this point. My arm shook as I pointed towards the front door. For a moment after Ted was gone, I thought I had overreacted, but I shook my head of that thought. If I felt a certain way, it was for a reason. Ted was out of line to tell me who I could and couldn't spend time with. If he had an issue with Jacob, that was on *him* and not me.

"Are you okay?" asked Jacob.

I sighed and proceeded to the table. "Yes. I will be." I took a seat at the table, peering over at the front door. "This isn't like him."

Jacob grimaced. "You remember your last relationship, right?"

I knew he was talking about Phil. Things started out nice, but once we moved in together, he had turned into a monster. Maybe he was always a monster, and I didn't see it until I was around it twenty-four seven. Nonetheless, I left that relationship with three broken ribs and a black eye. I hugged my arms and frowned. "This isn't him." I shook my head. "I… It's just not."

"You said that about Phil too."

I stared at Jacob. "With Phil, I made excuses for him. With Ted, I'm not."

Jacob raised his eyebrows, which made me roll my eyes.

"Things are happening here that are making me think this is more than just the typical abusive boyfriend story."

Jacob furrowed his brow. "Like what?" He put down the papers he was holding and focused all his attention on me.

"Ted is sleepwalking, and his nightmares seem to be getting worse." I paused as I debated telling him more. "Also, I heard something one night."

"What?" Jacob seemed genuinely curious.

I hugged my arms closer around me. "A growl along with scratching, and Ted went through these same experiences at that house. They still haunt him. There's more to the story I haven't told you." I swallowed as I fought over telling him everything. Would he find me crazy? Would he think I was excusing Ted's behavior? "I know how crazy this is going to sound, and at first, I didn't quite believe it either until that night I heard the loud growl." Sighing, I let it all spill out. Everything Ted had told me I said to Jacob, and as I did so, I watched his face to gauge his reaction. Did he think I was full of it?

When I finished the summary of Ted's life over the last three years, he stared down at the books and papers set out before him on the table. He didn't blink as he thought. "Hmm…." He was silent for a moment longer, and I pulled and itched at my fingers as I waited for his response. "This changes my line of thinking a bit in regards to the case because…" He dug through his hand-made notes. "Because it seems Dr. Ransteen was displaying some of the same anger issues as Ted. If you look at the notes here, you can see the change in his tone just by his writing." He flipped to a page that was dated December 12, 1892. "You see he is fine as he is discussing his everyday life. He discussed how his studying was going with the brain, and how he sent money to his brother. It was just a calm day for him. The following day was the same, and he expressed some concern for his mother, who seemed to be showing early signs of dementia or some kind of mental illness. Then there's this…" Jacob turned the page, and the date was scribbled haphazardly at the top. There were foreign symbols scribbled all along the paper over his original diary entry. The ink was dark against the paper, which made me suspect he wrote this in a fit of rage and pressed too hard on the paper. Jacob said, "This is a total change in behavior. He's talking about anger at things like a bird not shutting up, his brother's letter, and anger at his mother. His mood changes entirely. It is like this throughout the entire book." Jacob dug through some of the older papers and picked one up, scanning it with his eyes. "Ted's angry a lot nowadays, huh?"

I let out a breath. "Very. Ted isn't like this usually, which is why I thought it was PTSD or depression. Maybe both. I've known him for years working with him, and it was as if he took a dramatic turn."

Jacob looked over the papers. "I think there may be more to the story than these notebooks are giving."

When Jacob left after some time, I decided to give Ted a call to see where he was. I had cooled down finally and was willing to see his face again. However, whenever I called, he didn't pick up. Assuming he was with one of his friends, I decided I'd try to contact him again later.

I took a seat at my work table on the other end of the living room. It was where I kept my gems, jewels, and other accessories to decorate my seashells. Every few months, I drove to the beach to collect them after the tide went down. It was a relaxing hobby of mine, and I sold them online as an excellent way to make some extra cash. Every month I had a new theme, like witches for Halloween or little elves for Christmas.

The busier my hands were, the better my anxiety became. It was as if moving my fingers around dispelled the anxious energy built up inside my head. The concentration distracted me from all my anxious thoughts about Ted and life in general, which never seemed to go away. Before I knew it, I finished two seashells dressed like turkeys for the upcoming holiday. My procrastination never seemed to last because the cesspool of anxiety always made me want to work more.

Before I knew it, the sun was beginning to set, and Ted still wasn't home. I decided to give him another call, and instead of a few rings followed by a voicemail, it went straight to voicemail.

That was odd.

The constant pool of anxiousness began to bubble. What if something happened to him? I took a deep breath. Maybe he still needed time to cool off. I fumbled with my cell phone in my hand, squeezing the case off and on it. My nervousness can't get the best of me, because it often did.

It was late in the evening when I heard the keys outside the front door to our apartment jingle. I sat up on the couch where I now sat watching television. Ted opened the door and shut and locked it behind him. "Ted," I said as I got up and walked towards him, "where were ya all day?"

Calmly and in a neutral, almost monotone voice, he said, "For a walk."

My forehead creased. "A walk for almost eight hours?"

"Yes."

I wanted to gauge how he felt by looking into his eyes, but they were glazed over with no emotion. "Are you high?"

"No," he said in that same lifeless tone.

Concern seeped into my voice as I fumbled with my fingers. "Are you okay?"

"Yes."

That was a damn lie, but he wasn't giving me many answers. "Are you hungry?" I asked, going towards the fridge to warm up leftovers for him.

"No." Ted took a seat at the kitchen table. Even his posture was strange to me. He sat up straight with his hands placed neatly on his thighs. He stared straight ahead at nothing.

Was this some strange form of passive aggression? I put my hands on my hips. "Teddy, are you actin' like this 'cause you're mad at me?"

"No," said Ted in his zombie-like voice.

I dropped my hands at my side. "Oh… Okay. Um…" I thought of what I could do to help snap him out of this. Walking over towards him, I put a hand on his cheek. He didn't respond at all to my touch. I put my hand down and stared at him. "Ted?"

"Yes?" Ted turned to me. His eyes were lifeless. His face—expressionless. Ted was like a zombie.

I pulled on his arm and said, "Let's go sit on the couch and watch our favorite show."

"No."

I continued to tug on him. "Please?"

Without a word, he got up and sat on the couch with me, but it was as if he wasn't even watching the television. He stared in that general direction, but his eyes were too hyper-focused on the TV itself and not the entertainment on the screen. I hardly watched the episode because my focus was primarily on Ted's odd behavior.

An hour later, Ted got up and went towards the bedroom door. His movement wasn't hostile or even lazy. It was like that of a robot. When he went to open the door, it was so delicate, like touching air, as he gently pushed it open. The door didn't close in the typical heavy way Ted would close it. It was soft with a subtle click.

Sitting on the couch, I was shocked. What was wrong with him? A shiver ran down my spine as I thought about the possibility of how that house could be affecting him somehow. Whoever was in that bedroom, it wasn't Ted. I didn't feel right going to bed with that… stranger. Deciding to stay up, I settled myself on the couch for the night. I stayed up past midnight, watching television until I could no longer keep my eyes open.

During the middle of the night, I was stirred awake by the sound of rustling. It sounded like the utensils in our kitchen drawer being rifled through. Fear made my blood run cold. I was afraid of what I'd see if I sat up, but I swallowed it down. It could be Ted. He didn't eat when he got home.

Maybe he was hungry and getting something to eat. Perhaps he was back to his old self after some rest.

I sat up from the couch and saw Ted standing with perfect posture in the kitchen. "Ted?" I called.

No answer.

"Teddy?" I slowly stood up. He didn't move a muscle as I made my way over to him. Once I walked closer towards him, I realized he was holding a knife in his hand. It was one of the big knives we used for cutting meat and large vegetables. His eyes were wide open, but they were glazed over, still staring blankly at nothing. I could tell by how his arms flexed and his jaw muscles tightened that he was tense. His muscles were so tight he was almost shaking. "Ted?" My hands shook as I reached out to touch his arm. Maybe my touch would bring him back to reality.

My touch did the trick, and he blinked and stared down at his hands. The glazed over look was now gone. He blinked again and dropped the knife on the counter. His eyes now wide with what looked like fear, he took a step back. His face was ashen.

"Teddy, sweetie," I said, wanting to comfort him. I reached out to grab his hands.

Finally, he saw me for the first time since this morning. His eyes were frantic as he stared at me and then at the knife on the counter. "Wh-what's happening to me?"

I embraced him, and his whole body shook in my arms. My heart ached in pain. "Teddy…" I squeezed lovingly.

"Wh-what's happening to me?" His voice shook as he rested his head on my shoulders.

A warmth soaked up my shirt, and I realized he was crying. His wet tears and hot breath made me run my fingers through his hair. "I don't know, hon, but we're going to find out." Lifting his head, I stared into his eyes. His face was pained, and the tears soaked his cheeks. I had never seen him this way; it was disconcerting. "I promise. Ya goin' to be fine." I kissed his lips, and he kissed me back with fervor.

We held one another, and it was a relief knowing I had Ted back. The gentle Teddy I fell in love with. His touch was always so soft and kind, and it made me feel safe. We rested our foreheads against one another and continued to caress each other. "I don't think I can go back to sleep," said Ted.

"I know," I said. "Me neither."

Ted held on to me tightly. "Let's stay up and make it a late-night movie night or something. We can go get some Taco Bell or something while we're at it and try to make this fun." He sighed. "Anything to forget about all that's going on."

It was rare to have good moments with him nowadays, so I wanted to take advantage of it. We got food through the drive-thru and made our way home to set up shop on the couch. We started a light-hearted movie, and Ted held me as we attempted to relax. I could tell by the way Ted repeatedly rubbed his thumb over my knuckles and how he ground his teeth, he still felt tense. Halfway through the movie, I passed out. I wasn't much of a sleepover buddy.

In the morning, I woke up to the smell of bacon. My eyelids were still heavy from exhaustion, and now my neck hurt from sleeping on it funny all night. I slowly turned my neck side-to-side to massage out the cramp, and I winced as it slowly untwisted.

Ted sat at the kitchen table, drinking a cup of coffee, and scrolled through his phone. "Morning," he said after taking a sip.

"Are you doing okay today?" I asked slowly.

Ted looked up at me, and I let out a breath of relief when I saw his eyes were not zombie-like. "Yeah. I'm doing good today," he grimaced.

Was this going to be a habit of ours now? Me wondering if he was in a good mood or not and then walking around on eggshells? I could tell by Ted's downcast eyes, he was thinking the same thing and wasn't happy about it.

He let out a heavy sigh. "I'm going to get that prescription today."

Grabbing ahold of his hand, I pressed my lips tightly together. "I don't think that's going to fix anything, hon. I think what's going on is more…" I tried to find the right word for it. "Otherworldly than this."

Ted peered into my eyes. His brow furrowed in what I could only assume was fear. He whispered, "Yeah."

"Maybe we need to take a different route in this, ya know? For sure, therapy and medicine would help because this is some crazy stuff, but we should also seek other healing avenues. It has something to do with that house. I know it. Maybe finding a way to release ya from it would help."

Ted shrugged and ran his fingers through his hair. "I don't know, Christina. I just don't know." His shoulders were hunched over in defeat, and that made me lunge towards him and wrap him up in my arms.

"I have work today, but I'll come straight home right after," I said.

"Do you think you can handle a shift? We didn't get much sleep."

I smoothed my hands over his hair and kissed his forehead. "Yes. I'll be fine."

At work, all I could focus on was Ted. I sat behind the front desk, waiting to greet anyone who entered, but my game was off. I kept losing my pens, forgetting what I was doing, and not being my usual cheerful self with the clients and their families. My shift droned on longer than usual even though I was working my typical hours. I was beyond exhausted all day, and I found myself spacing out at the wall when given the spare time.

Once my shift was over, I raced out that door wanting to get home to Ted and see how he was doing. My thoughts were entirely obsessed with him and fixing him. By the time I got home, Ted was sitting at the kitchen table with Jacob and Ben. I tilted my head to one side as I stared at them. "What's goin' on?" I asked. It was strange of Jacob to be here without calling to tell me first. I saw Jacob's wide-eyed stare and Ted and Ben's ashen faces. Ted was so pale I thought he was going to pass out. "What's wrong?" I asked, worried.

"I've got some news. I'm not sure if I entirely believe it, but…" Ted paused. "With everything Ben has been telling me about what Monica gave him before she died, it's becoming increasingly more difficult to deny."

"Deny what?" I asked as I made my way over to the table.

Ted swallowed hard. His lips were so dry I could see they were cracking.

I darted my eyes back over to Ben and pulled at the ends of my sweater's sleeves. "Just tell me. You're making me nervous." My stomach began to churn in knots.

Jacob, Ben, and Ted exchanged glances. "Ben…" Jacob began.

"I'm possessed," finished Ted.

I blinked, frozen in place. "What?" Was that even possible?

Ben scooted his chair closer to the table. "I know that's hard to follow, but let me explain. Monica left behind books for me."

"I reached out to him today because of what he said the other night after we left the bar," said Ted.

"Monica was studying the occult before she died," said Ben. "And she took these notes." He opened this book that had a wooden cover, which I found odd. The wood had aged terribly with parts of it splintering off. Inside the book were the same strange symbols from Dr. Ransteen's notebook, and beside them were translations in English. Ben said, "Monica was translating everything. These symbols are from a rare and ancient religion from back in the B.C.E. era. There is almost no information about it nowadays, and it's difficult to get involved in it since it's so scarce. It's some sort of dark witchcraft or something. Ancient witchcraft, before even today's form of witchcraft."

"What made you give Monica's book a look after all these years?" I asked.

Ben shrugged. "I was drunk, but not too drunk to remember what I brought up. You both looked so worried about what I was saying." He looked at both me and Ted. "And so I decided to give it a look, so I took it out of storage. Seeing it made me realize there was probably more to what was going on with Ted, and she told me to give it to Ted when it was time." He shrugged again. "I figured I'd just give it to him."

"After Ben approached me with this, Jacob came by," said Ted.

"With both Monica's translation and what you and Ted found in that secret room, the puzzle is starting to fit together," said Jacob. "Dr. Ransteen was doing dangerous and evil work. Possibly performing them on his patients."

My stomach dropped, and suddenly I needed to lay down because my head was swimming. Before, I wouldn't have bought into this occult stuff as much, but after what Ted experienced, and myself, I found myself unable to deny it was all real.

"You there, Christina?" asked Ben.

"Y-yes," I managed to mumble. "What else?"

"Dr. Ransteen was working on some kind of curse he started on the property," said Jacob. "I don't know what this curse does, but he put out some powerful energy surrounding the property. Somehow and for some reason, it latched onto Ted."

After a moment, I realized I was holding my breath, so I exhaled out before saying to Jacob, "Thanks. So what do we do about this? How do we stop this curse? Can we even do that?"

"We don't know," said Ben. "Monica didn't finish translating the whole book before she was killed, but she got to the part where it mentions the name of the curse. It's called the Captis Curse."

"What is that?" My body felt heavy, as though I might be pulled through the ground at any moment.

Ted let out an exasperated sigh. "We don't know. All we know is this seems to be the link between me, the house, and Dr. Ransteen."

Jacob said, "I think Ted is bound to Dr. Ransteen in some way because of this curse. Maybe it's Dr. Ransteen that is controlling Ted and making him sleepwalk, have these nightmares, and making him lash out suddenly."

Ted looked down at the ground and chewed on his bottom lip. His knuckles turned white as he clutched them tightly into fists.

I furrowed my brow. "How?" It was as if all my breath was pushed out of my body.

"That we don't know yet, and we don't know how to stop it," said Jacob. "But we're going to find out."

Chapter Five

Ted's Internal Battle

The weather started to get colder as autumn neared its end. Christina put on the heater and wrapped herself up in one of the knitted blankets my mother had made her before she died. It was the last Christmas we'd had as a family, and my mother had warmed up instantly to Christina. They spent every weekend together, and a small, childish part of me had felt as though I had been replaced. Christina clung to her mug of tea with both hands as she read her book.

"Hey," I said softly to get her attention. "Come here." I gestured with my hands for her to come closer. She put her cup down on the coffee table and snuggled up against my chest with my arms wrapped around her. I raked my fingers through her hair gently—kissing her along her face. Despite this moment, the anxiety of my circumstance clung and ripped at my heart. Staring blankly at the television, the heavy weight of what was happening dragged me down. Swallowing hard, I thought of what happened to Lavinia when Howard had been possessed by Dr. Ransteen. Was that going to be me? I balled my hands into fists. My nails dug into my flesh. I had to find a way to fight this, and I needed help fast before I did something I'd regret. Well, I wouldn't do it, but I'd still face the consequences of Dr. Ransteen's actions *through* me regardless.

I thought of Howard and how he was locked up now. It wasn't fair, but the law didn't recognize being possessed as a valid excuse. We needed to solve this and fast. Christina looked up at me and smiled softly. I kissed her lips. I had to do something in the meantime to keep my loved ones and me safe.

It was hard to fall asleep that night. Worried I'd end up sleepwalking, I stayed up on my phone watching videos with my headphones in. Christina was fast asleep beside me snuggled up underneath her pile of numerous blankets. She got cold quickly and insisted on five blankets plus the heater running.

The coffee was futile because it became increasingly difficult to keep my eyes open as they drooped heavily. After staying up five hours past my bedtime, I knocked out with my phone still in my hand. A nightmare followed soon after I closed my eyes.

I was standing outside my body in the dream. All the colors appeared to be dampened by a gray fog of some sort. I was attached to my body, but I had no control over it as I watched it stand up and move towards the kitchen. At first, I tried digging my feet into the ground to see if that'd stop my body, but nothing worked.

"It's too late," I heard a male voice say.

Too late? Too late for what?

I stood directly behind my body as if trapped there in the back. I tried to put my hands on my shoulders to stop myself, but it was as if I was made of lead and couldn't move. Trapped, I was forced to stand and watch as my body grabbed a knife from the kitchen drawer. Its blade shined against the moonlight.

"Stop," I cried.

Almost robotically, my body made its way into the bedroom where Christina lay bundled up in bed, completely unaware. "No! Stop!" I screamed.

My body raised its arm, and I wanted to look away as the knife struck down, but I couldn't. Whoever was controlling me wouldn't let me. Blood splattered across the walls. Christina's blood-curdling scream was all I could hear. I bellowed out in anguish.

Fight! Fight, Ted!

I had no idea how you fought something like this, but I mustered all the strength I could internally to imagine pushing myself to the front of my body. I figured if I was standing in the back, maybe I needed to be in the front. Right now, I was in the passenger seat, and I needed to hurry over and push the damn driver out the car door.

"It's too late," that same voice said again. "The Beast has you now like it had me."

No!

Blood.

A scream that turned into a gurgle.

I imagined pushing myself into my body. For a moment, it felt like I was tensing my muscles, but I couldn't be since my body was no longer in my control. Still, I felt exhausted. I imagined pushing my being into my body, and suddenly my eyes shot open.

I wasn't in bed. I was standing over the bed, staring down at Christina.

With a knife in my hand.

I stumbled back as I dropped the knife to the floor. Falling to the ground, I took panicked breaths. The rise and fall of my chest let me know I was in control now. My eyes darted along the walls and ceiling.

No blood.

I managed to stand up. My legs wobbled as I did so.

I let out a giant breath of relief when I saw Christina unharmed in bed. Falling to my knees, I embraced Christina in my arms. This stirred her awake. "Teddy? What's the matter?" she asked.

Tears rained down my cheeks, and I let out a whimper as I clung to her.

"Teddy!" Christina said, alarmed. Without question, she immediately smoothed her hands up and down my back, attempting to calm me. "Hon, what's wrong?"

Christina was in danger as long as I was under attack. I couldn't risk her getting hurt by my hand. "I'm losing too much control to stay here," I said.

"What?" Christina's eyes widened. She pushed herself out of my arms and stared into my eyes. "What do ya mean?" Her brow was furrowed.

I shook my head. The tears still stained my cheeks. "I-I…" I couldn't find the words for it, so I pointed at the knife that laid on the carpet.

She gasped. "Teddy. You sleepwalked again." She looked into my eyes. "Are you okay?"

"You're worried about me?" I almost laughed. "Of course you are."

She managed a smile. "Yes, Teddy. I want you to be safe and healthy. I don't want this happenin' to ya."

I shook my head. "I don't want to kill you."

She pressed her lips tightly together. She remained silent.

I needed to leave, and fast, before I did do something. Before it became real and not a dream. Standing up with my hands balled into fists, I marched over to grab my duffle bag and threw my clothes into it.

"What are ya doin', Teddy?" Christina got out of bed.

"I have to go before I hurt you. I can't risk that."

Christina raced over to me and gripped my arm. "No! We can fix this!"

My heart lurched at her words. I chewed on the inside of my cheek. "No, we can't," I said. "Not before I do something permanent."

"Teddy, please!" Christina pulled on my arm.

I let out a sigh that weakened me. My chest ached in pain. More than anything, I wished I didn't have to go. I paused and turned to her. Dropping my bag, I pulled her in for a hug. What would calm her the most right now was her knowing I still loved her and my leaving had nothing to do with my lack of that. I firmly pressed my lips against hers. "I love you so much," I said. "So much it hurts. That's why I have to go."

Christina stared at me wide-eyed and took a step back.

"We will solve this. We will," I said as I went into the bathroom to grab a few essentials. "But in the meantime, we have to separate."

Christina was shaking. I eyed her medication that sat in its usual spot in the bathroom and shoved it in her direction. "Your whole body is shaking. Take it."

Her teeth chattered. When they started to do that, I knew another panic attack was on the rise. It'd be the wrong time to leave, but if I didn't go now, I never would. I zipped up my bag.

"W-wh-where will y-you go?" she asked.

"To my parents' cabin." I kissed her forehead and held her close to me. This seemed to help calm her a bit. "I love you. Once we figure this out, I can come back. For now, for your safety, I have to go." I kissed her lips one last time before racing out the door, before I changed my mind.
Or before someone else changed it for me.

Throwing duffle bag into the truck, I turned the engine. It was the early morning before the sun rose, and it was sprinkling outside. The sky was overcast, which made the bleakness of it match my mood. I sped off towards the mountains. It was about a forty-five-minute drive Clinging to the steering wheel, I sped through the town, trying to get out as soon as possible. The looming darkness that often consumed me was becoming louder. The snake crept down my back, making my skin crawl, and I pressed down on the gas pedal, wanting to put as much distance between Christina and me as I could.

I pulled up to the property, and the cabin sat there in the dark, shrouded by tall pine trees. The lights were off, and the entrance was surrounded by mud from the moisture in the air. The cabin was lifeless compared to how it was not too long ago when my mother was alive. My chest twisted as my mother came to the forefront of my mind. My father couldn't bear to stay in it, but he also couldn't bring himself to sell it since it was my mother's favorite escape.

I got out of the truck and walked over to unlock the front door. All of us had a set of keys to the cabin if we ever needed to drop by for a visit. Once inside, I dropped my duffle bag by the small table next to the front door. I texted Christina first that I arrived safely, hoping she was doing okay.

I dusted off the couch by patting down on it before vacuuming it. Keeping myself busy, I got to work sweeping the wood floors and wiping down the counters. Once the home was touched up, I made my bed. The sun was beginning to break through the horizon, and I was beyond exhausted from the lack of good sleep from that night. However, I still found myself too nervous to fall asleep. What if *I* never woke up?

I walked over to the bookshelf, where my mother's books sat. All of them were unfinished with bookmarks midway or a quarter way through. The Alzheimer's made her keep almost everything incomplete. I sighed and plopped down onto the couch, staring at her books and her knitted doilies she'd insisted on placing on everything.
Instead of dreading the reason I was here, I decided to appreciate the opportunity to be alone to heal from my mother's death. My father always said a man's therapy was work, so I went outside in search of firewood. My boots crunched over the fallen leaves and pine needles that caked the mountain floor.

Picking up bundles of wood in various sizes, I brought them back to the giant log my father used to ax the firewood into pieces. I went into the shed and grabbed the ax. The blade was aged from overuse, and the wood handle was discolored after spending hours in the hot sun. Stabling a piece of wood onto the giant log, I raised my arms over my head holding the ax, and chopped the wood in half.

After the pieces were small enough, I brought in pieces of dried pine needles and thin branches in order to start the fire. Once I got the flame strong enough, I added larger pieces of wood and blew on them to get the flame to grow. Successfully making a fire had a way of making me feel accomplished and proud.

With the cabin warming up, I peered around the living room and kitchen area. I had forgotten to pack myself any food, so I took a quick drive over to the nearest corner store. I grabbed myself some cans of soup and snacks along with jugs of water.

Once back at the cabin, it was fully warmed by the fireplace. I sat on the couch as I ate a bag of chips. There used to be a television, but my father took that with him when he moved out. All there was left were the books; my father didn't want the reminder of her Alzheimer's by taking them. I didn't blame him.

The lack of sleep finally got to me, and I crashed earlier than normal despite my attempt to fight my sleep. I startled awake after some time, and the sun was still barely breaking over the horizon. I furrowed my brow, completely confused. Maybe I was only asleep for a couple of minutes, but my body felt heavy and my head groggy, which told me I must've been sleeping a long time. Maybe I slept a whole day and woke up the following morning. I checked my phone to see the time, but it wasn't turning on. I pressed the power button over and over to no avail.

Sighing, I threw my phone onto the couch. A strange ringing started to envelop my ears, and I shook my head trying to relieve myself of it. I ground my teeth together as the ringing got louder. It completely consumed my head, and I got up and raced out the front door of the cabin, hoping the sounds of nature would drown out the ringing.

I slammed open the door and nearly fell when I saw there was no outside. There was only a black abyss the cabin floated in. Staring around at the blank vastness of space, I blinked profusely, trying to force myself out of this dream. Everything felt so real and vivid as though I were awake. I pinched my arm hard enough the skin between my fingernails turned white. I winced at the pain, which was real.

Without knowing what to do, I took a step back and closed the door before locking it. I swallowed hard as I backed away from the door. My muscles were tense with fear, and I tried to take steady breaths that seemed far too labored than what was deemed normal.

Was I dead? Was this what death was like, and I was waiting to go to the other side? Did the cabin catch on fire somehow? I thought of Dr. Ransteen, and my heart stopped for a split second as ice shot through me, causing me to freeze in place. Was this another possession?

I had to find a way out. Every window faced out into the black abyss. The only idea I could gather was to try and wake myself up. I ran to the kitchen sink, hoping the cold water would suffice, but nothing came out as I turned the faucet. Opening the cabinet underneath the sink, I checked the pipes. I grabbed the screwdriver that sat in a basket there and unscrewed the pipe and ripped it out, but no water came rushing out. There was nothing there. Frustrated, I banged the pipe against the cabinet door, which caused it to break off.

I got up and threw the broken cabinet door across the living room, where it slammed against the window and shattered it. A black mist began to seep in through the opening. The air dropped to freezing. My body was damp with sweat as the adrenaline rushed through me. There was a scent beginning to fill the cabin. It was pungent, and my nostrils flared. It was an odd combination of moisture-filled air, like that of an overcast day when it was about to rain, mixed with the scent of rotting flesh.

Whatever that mist was, it couldn't be good, so I went to the tall bookshelf that stood next to the window and pushed it in front of the window. The aged oak scraped against the hardwood floors, but I managed to block it.

Despite the air feeling cold, my body was dripping with sweat. I lifted the end of my shirt and used it to wipe my face. Focused on an escape, I peered around the room some more. There *had* to be a way out, and maybe if I shocked my dream body, it'd be enough to wake my *real* body. I eyed the fire, which I now realized was just hot embers. The faint orange glow of the charred pieces of wood seemed like the only way to wake myself up.

I walked to the opposite side of the room, as far from the fireplace as I could get. Pressing my body against the wall, I braced myself for what I was about to do. I took a big breath in and out. Crunching my hands into fists, I ran towards the fire and threw my body towards it. The burning embers kissed my skin and left sharp, searing pain in its wake. My body shook from the agony, and I let out a yell as

I crumbled from the hot coals. I willed my body out of it, and the instant relief only lasted a second before the aftereffects of burning flesh left behind a throbbing burn. My cooked skin created a new smell of fresh rot. It was only after I yelled out in pain that I realized maybe I was awake this entire time and just hallucinating.

In agony, I continued to scream. After a while, I managed to calm myself and stayed on the cool floor. My body still sweat profusely. The blisters that formed on the left side of my body seethed as drops of sweat dripped over them. I clenched my teeth and let out another yell.

After a few moments of lying there, I heard a female's voice. "Ted." It was soft and inviting. I poked my head up from the floor to try to hear better.

"Ted," the woman's voice called out again. I recognized it from my previous dreams. I raised an eyebrow, curious as to who this unknown person was. It wasn't Christina's voice since it didn't have her accent.

It went silent again, so I called out, "H-hello?" My voice was hoarse, so I cleared my throat.

"Get up, Ted," said the woman. It didn't sound demanding. It was calming and strangely healing. "Ted. Get up."

So I did. I had no idea how I was able to get up since I felt so weak. The muscles in my body screamed and ached as I managed to will myself to stand.

"You have to leave, Ted," said the woman.

I swallowed hard as I eyed the door. It appeared menacing, as if mocking me. I knew the door led to someplace unknown.

Someplace dark.

I shook my head. "I can't."

The woman didn't reply, and it was silent again. The ringing in my ears returned, and I clasped my hands over them. The ringing turned into a high-pitched screeching similar to nails on a chalkboard, and I squeezed my eyes shut as I yelled out.

"Ted!" I heard the woman scream this time. The woman sounded closer now, and it was raspy. I knew this voice from somewhere.

The noise in my ears became deafening, and since I wasn't finding any solace inside the cabin, I decided to listen to the inviting woman's voice. I was already in hell, it seemed, so I might as well keep going. Stomping towards the door, I swung it wide open. The black abyss didn't have that wet, fleshy scent, but there seemed to be no air. It didn't make sense, but then again, my being in this space didn't either. As I took a step out of the cabin, I was fully expecting to start falling because it appeared as though there was no floor. However, as my foot found solid ground, I raised an eyebrow suspiciously—nothing about this made sense. There was nothing logical about this foreign place.

The cabin's door slammed shut behind me, and I jumped. I eyed the door handle, second-guessing my decision to leave the only familiar place. Before I could decide whether or not to re-enter, that same woman's voice called out, "Ted."

I whipped my head around. "Where are you? *What* are you?"

"Follow my voice," her voice echoed. It shimmered across the abyss.

I took a careful step forward and felt the ground with my shoe. After a few steps, it seemed the floor was steady, so I walked more confidently into the darkness. "Keep going," the woman's voice said. After several more minutes of walking and seeing nothing but blackness, the woman said, "You're almost there."

My body continued to sweat, and my tongue was now dry. My chapped lips cracked more as I continued deeper into the black hole. I ground my teeth together, utterly unsure of where I was or what I was doing. The fear in my heart made my blood run cold, but without any hope for an escape, I had to continue.

Suddenly, a new smell bombarded my nose. This time it was sweet with a touch of wood and spice. For the first time, I felt like I could breathe. I had no idea just how strained my lungs were until I could finally take a big enough breath in and out easily.

"Ted," said the woman. In the distance, I saw a glimmer of purple. The black mist distorted the image, but as it got closer, I made out flesh-colored lines like that of legs and arms. I would've been afraid if it weren't for the inviting scent. It seemed to calm me somehow and made me feel safe. "Ted," the shimmer said.

"What are you?" I called out. "Why are you in my dreams?"

"To help," it said.

"How? Where am I?" I peered around at the abyss.

"You are in the astral realm."

"The what?"

"It is where spirits live."

I panicked. My chest heaved up and down. Did this mean I was dead? "How did I end up here? Am I dead? How did I die?"

As it got closer, the way its hips swayed told me it was a woman. Her curly, black hair reminded me of Christina's when she didn't brush it. I looked into those familiar dark brown eyes and realized it was Lavinia. My eyes widened, and relief immediately rushed over me. Without thinking, I embraced her. I could have cried. Her touch felt warm and safe. My muscles relaxed, and my shoulders slumped over her. She was tall, so I didn't have to lean over as we hugged one another like I had to with Christina or my sister.

She patted her hand on my back. "Ted." I could hear the smile in her voice.

Lavinia's sister, Monica, came across my mind. Instantly, I was overcome with grief as it weighed heavily on my chest. I took a deep breath. "I'm so sorry for what happened to Monica. I tried. I-I…" My mind raced as I thought back to me and Monica's search for the truth about Lavinia's death and how Dr. Ransteen had killed Monica. "I'm sorry."

Lavinia shook her head and placed a finger to my lips. "It is okay. Everything is as it should be."

I furrowed my brow. How could she say that? Her sister died in such a gruesome way. Lavinia was murdered by her boyfriend who was possessed by Dr. Ransteen. How could any of this be as it should?

She smiled. "I know. I used to think the same thing when I was alive, but being a spirit gives you a broad perspective. One you cannot even fathom because you are stuck on Earth where you can only see what is happening immediately in front of you. Where you can only respond with short-sightedness because your earthly emotions consume you. This is okay." She smiled. "This is how Earth is supposed to be because you are there to learn and grow. You are growing in a way that is not often sought, but it is happening just as it should."

I shook my head. "I don't understand."

She smiled as she cupped the side of my face. "You will in time."

"How do I get out of here? Where is your sister?"

Her pleasant smile remained there. "Monica is healing."

My brow creased further. "Healing? What do you mean? She's alive?"

Lavinia's smile grew. "Yes, but that is only because death is an illusion. Like all souls, once we leave the physical realm, we must have a healing period. She is doing fine."

That's all I needed to hear, and I let out a breath of relief. All that mattered was Monica was now at peace and not trapped under Dr. Ransteen, even in death. "How do I get out of here?"

"In order to break free, you must first understand the basics. They will help aid you on your journey as you try to break free of the curse."

"What *is* the curse?" My breath quickened as the mention of it made my heart race.

"The land where the mansion was is haunted by a curse from the accumulation of negative energy there. When an event powerful enough takes place somewhere, it leaves an imprint on that land. Think of battlefields or asylums that are haunted. It is because a strong enough force took place there that left a permanent mark, like a scar on your body. Everything is made up of energy, including our thoughts and emotions, so when a strong enough force of energy like that curse is created, it cannot be destroyed. Energy never dies, which is why there is some form of existence even after our bodies have died. Energy can only be changed, so you must change the energy to free yourself. For some reason, the energy of the house latched itself onto you and now follows you beyond the house.

"Dr. Ransteen created such a powerful energy force that it was something close to a tornado, but unlike earthly tornadoes, this one stays in one place. This energy tornado created a portal. The curse that has formed stays in whatever location the portal has been opened. You must *change* the portal. You must change the direction of the tornado because the portal cannot be destroyed. Its trajectory and its purpose can only be changed. Only light can combat the dark."

A headache formed as I tried to wrap my head around this energy nonsense. "This sounds like a fantasy."

Lavinia smiled. "Things oftentimes overlap. Nothing is plain black or white."

I spaced out, staring into the darkness as I tried to brainstorm how to fight this energy. How does one fight something they cannot see or touch?

Lavinia continued. "Light and dark are essential to our existence. Even in the afterlife. You cannot have light without dark and vice versa."

What Lavinia was speaking about reminded me of what Dr. Ransteen had told me about when he had me and my mother trapped in the basement of the old house. He said you couldn't have the light without the dark, and his darkness was needed to bring about positive change. His experiments were evil, but he said they were beneficial in the long run because it'd help find cures.

"The universe is always balanced, and positive and negative energy keeps that balance," said Lavinia. "Right now, the negative energy is too powerful within you and on that land. The curse is creating an off-balance, and only positive energy can restore a peaceful one."

I stepped away from Lavinia, completely confused. "How do I do that, though? I am angry all the time now." I thought of my outbursts and my depression. "How do I fight something that is obviously winning? How do I defeat something that has control over me!"

Lavinia was quiet as she let me yell before she responded. "There are two worlds of existence. The astral realm is where you go in your dreams. Your nightmares and every dream is in astral. You have been traveling to this realm for some time. Everyone does throughout their entire life. That is why dreams feel so real, because they are. But your astral realm is now being controlled by what Dr. Ransteen started. The astral realm is where you are now. The physical and astral both coexist as one." She laced her fingers together. "I can slip in and out of the physical realm whenever I like as a spirit, but so can you as someone who is in a physical body. In the astral realm, you can manipulate energy easier. It is why we dream of the things that bother us the most in our waking lives. It is so we can work through our emotions, because it is easier. This curse is much too strong to do anything in the physical. You must defeat it in astral."

I raked my fingers through my hair. "How do I do that?"

Lavinia shook her head. "You are too weak, and more answers must be found. Dr. Ransteen is not the true person who has you. It is something much bigger than him. Christina..." She smiled. "She is working hard to help you."

I ripped at my hair. "I don't want her to get hurt." My anxiety pulled at my chest and labored my breathing.

"She won't," said Lavinia calmly.

I let out a breath and bent over, relieved. "Thank you... Thank you."

"For now, I will help you out of this place."

Pulling my shoulders back and standing up straight, I nodded. I was ready to escape. I was prepared to destroy whatever this was. Lavinia put her hand to my heart, and I felt a sudden warmth. It wasn't hot. It was calming and made my sweating cease. Every muscle in my body relaxed, and it felt like a strong force of energy rush through me. "I'm giving you a piece of my spirit to give you strength," she said.

I nodded as I grabbed onto her wrist. Closing my eyes, I took a deep breath in, inviting in the energy to envelop me more. For a moment, I felt silly, but the strength I could feel soaking up my veins made me believe in the whole idea of energy.

"You have been cursed for some time. All your anger, even when you were living in the home, was all the curse."

I thought back on the anger towards my father and our physical fights. We'd never fought like that before until I moved into that house. I thought of my need for control over my mother and her illness, and that was when it dawned on me this entire time I had been possessed.

It was as if Lavinia knew I hit this epiphany, and she nodded her head. "Yes. You have been under its control for some time, but hope is not lost. You will get through this. You have the right people by your side this time."

Lavinia's energy continued to swarm through me like an electric current. It was almost intoxicating, and my whole body began to buzz from it. For a split second, the power of it frightened me, to which Lavinia told me to take a deep breath. That made it easier for my body to surrender to the surge of electricity that coursed through me.

"Think of things that empower you. As clichéd as it sounds, love is the most powerful form of energy. Think of things that bring you love and joy," said Lavinia.

Thoughts of my mother danced through my mind along with my sister, my friends at work, the patients I cared for and the ones that had passed, and finally, of Christina. A smile broke across my face, and an overwhelming feeling of love bloomed in my chest and heated me up. The warmth swam across my body, and when I opened my eyes, I stood in the cabin again. The afternoon sun danced across the wood floors and paneled walls of the cabin. I patted my chest and arms to make sure it was me that was in control and let out a sigh of relief.

Chapter Six

Christina's Search

I fumbled the plastic bottle in my hand as I twisted open the cap. Shoving one of the small, white pills into my mouth, I swallowed.

Ted was gone.

My panic made my chest constrict, and I gripped tightly to my shirt. I fell to my knees as I gasped for breath, and my throat felt as though it were swelling shut. What if something happened to him? What if I couldn't fix this? What if Ted never came back as *himself*?

Lyingthe floor next to the bathroom, I curled into a ball as I choked on a nonexistent swollen throat. I knew it was my anxiety, but I couldn't stop my body from reacting to it. After fifteen minutes, my anxiety meds kicked in, and my breathing slowed. It felt like an hour had gone by before I got up and managed to make my way back into bed. All the while, my legs wobbled and my knees found it challenging to keep me up as I crawled underneath the blankets.

I called in sick to work that day because my medication made me unable to be fully aware. It rid me of my panic attacks, but at the same time, it made me groggy and unable to function.

The rest of my day was spent in bed. At one point, my stomach growled from hunger, so I forced myself up to eat a banana. "There," I said, looking down at my stomach. "You happy now? Can you shut up?" I sat on the couch as I stared blankly at the wall. I felt nothing.

No happiness, joy, fear, or anger.

I was just a shell of a person, which was welcomed at a time like this.

I had no idea how much time had passed, but my phone ringing from the bedroom was enough to snap me out of my trance. The phone's ringtone blared as I trudged over to the nightstand by my bed. I had missed the call by the time I got there, and I checked the caller ID.

It was Jacob.

Lying in bed, I dialed his number. "Hey," I said in a sleepy voice. "Sorry for missin' your call."

"Are you okay?" I could hear the worry in his voice.

I sighed. "Yeah." I rubbed my face. "Just anxiety. My meds make me sleepy."

"Oh." He was quiet for a second. "I-I can call back if this is a bad time…"

"No, no," I said without any sense of urgency. "What's goin' on?"

"After meeting Ben, I decided to keep in contact. He and I have been working on translating that wooden book from Monica. I think we may have figured something out, but you should rest."

The thought of finding a solution for Ted shot me awake. I rubbed my eyes. "No! Come over," I said. "I have something to share with you too."

After we hung up, I pushed the covers off of me and started the coffee pot. I stood in the kitchen, drumming my fingers on the counter as I tried to blink away the drowsiness. This couldn't go on. All this stress was too much on both of us, and we have missed a lot of work. It was a good thing we both had savings that would last us months just in case we lost our jobs, but there was no way we could continue this kind of life. Jacob and Ben were my best bet at finding a solution. Where did you go for a possession? A church? A shaman?

I ran my fingers through my hair and lightly tugged. Letting out a deep sigh, I trudged to the bathroom to start a shower. Standing there in our small, cramped shower, I let the warm water hit my face. It was refreshing and brought some life back into my eyes. I rubbed them further and stayed in the shower a little longer than usual.

Getting myself dressed in comfortable clothes, I managed to brush my thick hair. The brush got stuck at times in the curly knots. I let out a sharp breath of frustration as I settled for putting it up with a scrunchy.

As I sipped on my coffee, I saw Ted's text that he had arrived safely. I clutched my phone and closed my eyes, not wanting the tears to fall. They did anyway, and the frustration, fear, and hopelessness that had been building up for the past couple of weeks all came pouring out with each drop of liquid. My mama always said a good cry could fix anything, so I sat there at the table—my head resting on the soft, wooden top—shedding my emotions through tears.

It wasn't often I cried, but I found myself in this position every once in a while when things got too rough. It felt releasing, and the air around me lifted. As I wiped at my nose with my sleeve, I couldn't help thinking my mama was right. A good cry was all you needed sometimes.

A soft knock came at my apartment door. I quickly wiped the tears from my cheeks and sniffled before getting up to open the door. Jacob stood there, holding a soft-bound leather briefcase. When he saw me, his head titled slightly to one side, and his forehead creased. "What's wrong?" he asked.

Shaking my head, I said, "Get in. I'll explain."

He stepped inside and asked, "Is Ted at work?"

I locked the apartment door. "No. I have a lot to tell ya."

Right then, there was another knock. It was Ben.

He took a glance at me and said, "Woah! What the hell happened to *you*?"

"Just sit down," I said exasperated.

"What's going on?" asked Ben.

"Take a seat," said Jacob, motioning to the chair beside him.

Ben's forehead was pinched in concern.

I sighed as I took a seat across from them. I chewed on my bottom lip and fidgeted with the end of my sleeves. "Ted had to leave."

Ben's eyes widened. "What happened?"

Jacob sat up in alert. "Are you okay?"

Shaking my head, more tears threatened to come out. I blinked them away. "There's somethin' wrong with him, and he and I both know it. He left for my safety. Last night…" I paused. "He had been sleepwalkin' lately, and last night he was sleepwalking with a knife."

Jacob leaned back in his chair and eyed me warily. "What?"

Ben breathed out. "Fuuuuuck."

"I know how this sounds." I let out a breath. "I know, but his nightmares have gotten worse, and he doesn't recall ever gettin' up. He has lost all control."

Ben's mouth fell open. "This is a trip. I've been working on translating, but it's hard. I think it's Latin, but it listed some symptoms of this Captis Curse."

Jacob and I eyed Ben.

Ben shrugged. "What? It's what I'm calling it now. You gotta add some humor to things. Anyway, I managed to find that the victim of this curse would often exhibit certain symptoms, like sleepwalking, and when they did, they'd find the nearest weapon. That's when most people ended up killing others while in that trance-like state."

My heart dropped and my blood ran cold. "I could have ended up like Lavinia."

Jacob nodded. "And Ted would have been locked up for a crime he didn't technically commit, like Lavinia's boyfriend."

I stared at the table as my thoughts swam. "This is all so crazy."

Jacob reached a hand out and grabbed my arm to console me. "I know. It is for me too, but we're here to help. Hopefully, we can translate the rest of Monica's book. Maybe it'll have the solution to rid Ted of this thing."

My face scrunched up as I began to cry again. "I just want my Teddy back."

Jacob squeezed my arm lovingly. "I know."

Ben added, "I'm surprised Dr. Ransteen isn't more in the mainstream in regards to serial killers. There seems to be little to no information on him other than he ran an asylum in that house. It makes me wonder what other serial killers have fallen through the cracks in the past."

Jacob said, "Well, we didn't quite have the technology we do now. It's much harder to get away with murder nowadays."

"There is something else," said Ben. "There seems to be a lot of reference to the Beast of Eternal Life. Do you know anything about that?"

I nodded. "Yeah. Ted told me Dr. Ransteen had made a deal with some kind of demon who was called by that name so he could be immortal on Earth, but what does that have to do with Ted's possession and curse? Isn't it Dr. Ransteen we're worried about?"

"Perhaps," answered Jacob.

"We won't know much of anything until we translate everything. We'll have to find someone that knows Latin and these symbols."

I took the wooden book. It was rough, and the pages were thicker than normal paper. "Can I have this for now? I'd like to take a crack at it."

"Go for it!" said Ben.

Jacob hesitated before nodding. "Okay. Want me to stay with you tonight? I can bring Deidre over, or you can come over to our place for dinner. She's been worried about you."

I mulled it over. For some reason, some part of me felt like I had to be alone and afraid like Ted must be feeling right now. However, I knew that was nonsense. The fact was I needed to be surrounded by people. At least until I could get Ted back. "You think she could make some good southern cookin'?" I managed to give a smile.

"I sure can call and ask," Jacob said.

"I can help, but I miss the food of home."

Jacob chuckled. "She *does* make the best creamed corn now, thanks to your recipe."

My mouth watered at the thought of it. The last time I had that was last year during Thanksgiving. "Yes! I need some comfort food."

"I'm sure she'd be more than happy to oblige. It's only noon, so you both got some time to get cooking."

I let out a laugh. It felt good to laugh. "Oh, you're helpin' too!"

"You can tag along too, Ben," said Jacob.

Ben rubbed his belly. "A home cooked meal sounds good."

I left with Jacob in his car, and Ben followed behind us over to Jacob's home, which was on the outskirts of town. They always preferred seclusion, but they didn't want to be too far from civilization. That's why Saratoga Springs was perfect for them. Jacob taught a class once a week at Columbia University, but he didn't mind the commute.

While on the way to his house, Jacob gave his wife a call. "Hey, babe," he said. "I've got Christina with me." He let out a chuckle. "She's going to eat dinner with us along with a new friend I made. Is that good?"

I could hear her muffled voice through the phone. Her voice got high-pitched with excitement, and she said,

"Of course! I bet she'll want food that reminds her of home. I'll head to the store to get some catfish!"

The thought of catfish made my mouth water, followed by a deep sorrow that made my chest ache. I missed home.

Jacob pulled up to his house, a nice single-story place surrounded by tall trees to provide ample shade. Luscious green grass took up the half-acre plot which the house sat at the back of. A fence surrounded their land. Soft gravel surrounded the house once you pulled off the main road. The home was welcoming with its large bay windows in front and the rose bushes Deidre tended to.

Seeing the roses reminded me of Deirdre's green thumb. "How did she fare in the rose competition this year?" I asked.

Jacob unbuckled himself. "Great! She got second place this year."

"Good for her," I said. "She's been working hard at it."

"She gets better every year."

Jacob unlocked the front door, and I stepped inside. Their home was modest and beautiful. There was pebble-tiled flooring that covered the entryway area. Jacob set his keys and briefcase down by the table near the front door. He took off his jacket and hung it up on the coat rack nailed to the wall.

To the left was the carpeted living room, and to the right was the hallway that led to the bedrooms. A second living room area and dining room ahead of me passed the half-wall connected to the kitchen.

Since Deidre was still gone at the store, I decided to use this time to cipher through the wooden book I brought along. "Can I use your computer, Jacob?" I asked.

Jacob logged me in, and I searched for paranormal and occult forums. I used my phone to take pictures of the book to upload onto the computer. In every forum I could find, I made a post and uploaded the pictures asking for help with translations.

After a while, I stepped out into their back patio and gazed over the sunlight that hit their pool. Ben was seated, holding a glass of iced tea. "Did you find a translator?" he asked.

"Not yet," I said taking a seat beside him in the wicker chair.

Ben took a sip of his drink. After a moment, he said, "Life is crazy."

I laughed a little. "I know."

"I didn't know Monica long before she died," he said. "But she was spectacular. I was so scared of her in the beginning." He smiled.

I giggled. "I remember ya used to hide from her at work."

Ben laughed. "I was intimidated by her beauty, man. I didn't want to make a fool of myself like I always do."

"She found you adorable, I'm sure," I said.

Ben gave me a cheeky grin. "We had a nice thing going, but life can be surprising." His smile vanished, which made me frown too. "It made me realize I had to do more with my life, you know? She was so full of adventure and not afraid. I wanted to be more like that." He took a drink. "I'm trying. I had a dream about her a few nights ago, and she was just smiling. The whole time. She was just there smiling with that black hair and pale skin of hers. I woke up and knew I had to face my grief. That's what truly made me get that wooden book out of storage. *She* did."

The sun's light hit right in front of my eyes, and I used my hand to shield myself from it. "Ya really loved her."

Ben sighed. "Yeah... I did, which is stupid because we'd barely started dating. I don't know what it was, but I fell for her fast."

That made me smile.

"Like Ted did with you. He was all googly-eyed for you."

I giggled.

Ben took another drink. He was quiet, and I could tell he was thinking. His eyes seemed so far away. "That was my first dream about her too, and I woke up wanting more. Every night I look forward to sleep and a chance of seeing her." He looked over at me. "It felt so *real*. Like she was actually there."

"My mama always said our loved ones visit us in dreams because that's where our world and theirs meet. It's easier for us to see them and hear them."

Ben puckered his lips and let out a slow breath. "Yeah." He fell silent.

Shortly after, Deidre came home. I heard her holler from the kitchen. "Christina! Get over here!" she yelled. I excused myself from Ben and went into the kitchen. She squealed with excitement as she set down her bags of groceries and made her way over to embrace me. She tilted us side to side as she held me in her arms. "I *missed* you!" she said. Deidre's smile was stunning, and it always had a way of making you smile in return, even if you didn't feel like you could muster it. Her laugh had the same effect. She broke the hug and clapped onto my shoulders. "We're having blackened catfish for dinner. I need help with the sides."

I nodded my head. "I can help."

"Good!" Her hips swayed as she made her way back towards the kitchen. "With work and writing, I don't cook much anymore, so this is a nice change of pace."

Deidre worked for a nonprofit organization based out of the big city, but she worked from home. On the side, she wrote novels. She pulled out a bottle of wine and twisted it open. "Let's drink!" she said with a huge smile. She had her afro pulled back with the headband I had knitted for her. I was always jealous of her hair. It was so lush and beautiful. Any hairstyle she tried looked amazing on her.

The backyard door slid open, and Ben stepped inside with his empty glass of tea.

"Hi there," said Deidre. She walked over to him. Her heels clacked against the pebbled floor. "My name is Deidre. I'm Jacob's wife. You are this new friend of his?"

Ben shook her hand back. His cheeks were pink, and he gave a shy smile. "Yeah. We met through Christina. I'm a good friend of Ted's."

Deidre lifted an eyebrow. "Oh, really? This infamous Ted. Come take a seat, Ben. Us ladies will want some extra help in the kitchen."

Ben put his hands into his pockets. His cheeks were still flushed. "Sure thing."

I eyed the plastic tapestry that hung over a newly knocked-out wall behind Deidre. She looked over her shoulder to look at it and then back at me. "We're expanding the house," she said. "We thought of moving, but we are *so* close to paying off the mortgage we decided not to. Plus, I love this property." She poured me and her a small glass of wine before offering some to Ben.

"Sure, why not?" he said.

I took a seat at the barstool at the island counter with Ben. "It'd be nice to own something outright like a house, you know?" she said.

I nodded my head.

"Plus, we are thinking of having kids soon."

I got a huge grin on my face. "Your babies would be so stinkin' cute!"

"I know that!" she said with a wink.

I let out a sigh of relief. It was nice to get away from all the chaos that was now my life, and the great thing was Deidre knew not to bring it up. She knew by now if I wanted to talk about it, I'd say it.

We discussed going back to our hometowns to see our families as we started making dinner. Deidre came from a large family like me. She was the only girl in a house full of five boys. "I miss my brothers," she said.

"How are they doin'?"

"Good." She immediately refilled my and Ben's wine glasses when they got too low.

We prepped everything first, and I was getting everything ready to make the rice, which was my specialty. I used my grandmother's Cajun recipe for it.

"My youngest brother graduated high school," she said.

"Good for him. Is he going to college?"

"He better!" She laughed. "He is taking a year off." She rolled her eyes. "I don't understand that, but hey… It's not my life. Just get started on your success, you know? Why wait?"

I nodded. "Maybe high school wiped him out."

She scoffed. "No excuse."

"How's your mom?"

Deidre's lips fit into a tight line. "Not too good. Her cancer came back."

I clicked my tongue. My heart deflated. "I'm so sorry, Deidre."

"Yeah, I know. I offered to pay for her chemo, but she's so prideful." She shook her head before shrugging. "But what are you gonna do, you know? She's strong. She'll be fine."

I put a hand on Deidre's shoulder.

Ben helped with chopping up some of the vegetables. "I know how hard that can be. I'm real sorry about that. My father died of cancer."

"What did he have?" asked Deidre.

"Bone cancer."

Deidre and I tsked.

"It's what drove me to pursue a career in the medical field. I work with Christina at the nursing facility."

Deidre grinned, and I noticed it made Ben blush even more. He always got bashful around beautiful women. "Oh that's nice! Are you wanting to work there for long or…?"

"I'm working through the nursing program at the local hospital."

"Good for you."

Ben took a sip of wine. His face was beet read. "Thanks."

Jacob came into the kitchen. "My wife got you working for her, huh?" he said to Ben.

"A man can help around the kitchen too, and he should," said Deidre pointing the cooking spoon at him.

"I don't mind it," added Ben.

"Come on, Ben, let me show you my new pool table," said Jacob. Ben got up and left out of the kitchen.

Deidre playfully rolled her eyes. "We're gonna eat without them. On to a more important topic, we need to figure out what to do with that hair of yours."

I let out a laugh and my cheeks warmed. "I know. Today was *not* a good hair day."

"Is it ever a good hair day for you?" she teased.

My smile grew. "Shut up. Not all of us can have perfect hair like you."

She patted her hands on her afro dramatically and fluttered her eyes. "I know. I'm blessed. I'm telling you that you need to start using the same products I do. Pantene won't cut curly hair like yours. Let me show you what I buy." I followed her out of the kitchen and to the bathroom.

"I get my curly hair from my mom's side. Hers is much worse than mine," I said.

"Your natural curls are beautiful," she said, pulling at the strands.

"As you know, my mom's family is from Mexico, so I got her genetics when it came to hair."

"How did your parents meet?" Deidre asked me.

"My grandmother moved to California from the south to marry my grandfather, who is from there. His family had

132

immigrated there from Mexico years before that. My mother ended up moving to the southern states for college since her mother had family there she could live with. That's where she met my father."

"I bet your great-great-grandparents just *loved* that their daughter married a brown man," said Deidre sarcastically.

I laughed nervously. "They were ecstatic," I said, returning the same dry sarcasm. Family get-togethers were still a little tense between my family and the "pure-blooded" Baileys, but I tried not to let it get to me. Deidre gave me some of her extra hair products to take home, and we went back to making dinner.

Jacob and Ben came out when we started the catfish. "It smells good," he said.

"Oh, *now* he comes out," said Deidre. Jacob leaned over to kiss her on the cheek. "You are cleaning afterwards."

"I know the drill," said Jacob grabbing a green bean to eat from off the stove.

We set the table when dinner was ready, and we finished off our bottle of wine during the meal. The laughter we shared over our meal made me feel a release of something heavy I hadn't known was there. It's strange how quickly we adapt and forget the negative emotions we've been carrying.

After dinner, we sat on the couch to watch some television. Before I knew it, it was ten at night. I yawned, which made Deidre do the same. "I think it's time I head out," I said. I looked over to Ben for confirmation, who nodded his head to show he was ready to go as well.

Deidre rested her head in her hand as she leaned her elbow against the back of the couch. "Okay," she said. "It was a pleasure having you here tonight. You should come over more often, and not just for holidays."

I nodded and nervously played at my sleeve. My anxiety meds were beginning to wear off. "Thanks. I will."

Ben gave me a ride home back to my apartment. Once inside, I called out for Ted, but nobody answered. My heart sank, and my once lifted mood quickly became heavy again from the weight of the reality I lived in. Taking another anxiety pill, I crawled into bed. I knew I wouldn't be able to fall asleep with everything going on, but the meds helped to knock me out.

My dreams were nothing but a black abyss. There was nobody and nothing to see but blackness that seemed to go on for an eternity. That was until I saw a young man appear from the fold of darkness. He wore brown pants with matching suspenders over a worn-out, white T-shirt. His hair was a bit unkempt, but he was otherwise clean and handsome looking. He said nothing. The man pointed off to the left of him. There was nothing there but blackness, so I decided to head in that direction.

I heard him say from behind me, "I know the answer."

I whipped around, and the young man was no longer there. Instead, an image formed of an elderly man in a wheelchair. He was hooked up to an oxygen tank, and he sat staring at a fireplace.

"I know the answer," said the male voice once again.

"What answer? To what?"

I shot awake from the sound of my phone going off. Rubbing my eyes, I shoved my curls out of my face. I picked up my phone and saw I had gotten an email. I let out a grunt, annoyed at myself for forgetting to turn off the notification sound on my phone. Since I was up, I decided to check what the email said. It was an update from one of the occult forums I'd posted to. My heart's pace quickened. I quickly opened up to see who replied.

A commenter named Black Raven said, "I studied Latin for years, and this seems a little different than the traditional Latin that I know. I can make out some of the words, but there is a lot on here that doesn't derive from the Latin language. I'm not sure what you have here, but it appears to be a dead language of some kind."

I sighed and held my head down.

Great.

Another dead end.

Chapter Seven

Too Late

I focused on my breathing because that was the only thing that seemed to be real. Blinking, I scanned the cabin making sure everything was real. There was no more black abyss through the windows. I opened the cabin door and gingerly stepped onto the dirt ground, half expecting to fall through it. At this point, anything was possible.

Once I realized I was indeed awake and back in the reality I was familiar with, I gazed up at the sky and closed my eyes to soak up the sun's rays. My body warmed, and the slight breeze from the autumn air was refreshing on my arms. When I remembered I ran into the fireplace, I studied my arms to check if the injuries were at all real, but there was nothing there. Going back inside the cabin, I looked underneath the sink. The pipe I broke in the dream was still attached. I turned on the faucet, and water came rushing out.

I rubbed my head. Last night sure was one hell of a dream. My sense of relief at being back was quickly overshadowed by this dark, cold energy that seemed to inch across my back. It sent a cold sweat through me, and I got goosebumps.

The invisible dark cloud inched its way up my spine and clouded my head, making a migraine pierce my brain. I winced as I grabbed onto my head. The snake-like cloud slowly enveloped me, and I felt like I was physically pulled down into the Earth.

That was when the whispers started.

I couldn't make out what they were saying, and it sounded like a series of voices. I tried to zone in on one voice to hear what it was saying, but I couldn't concentrate.

This couldn't be good.

I thought of what Lavinia said. Maybe the astral realm was the key to defeating this thing, but how could one fight a curse like this? Still, that dream, if it even was one, gave me a sense of hope again. It gave me back my fight. I sat up from the couch with my chest held high. It felt as though I had a sense of control over myself again. Suddenly, my cell phone rang, which made the voices cease.

It was Christina.

"Hello," I said.

"Ted, I had a dream," she said. "I was in this black abyss for hours."

Astral realm.

"And I saw this man. He had on brown pants and suspenders."

My heart dropped. I saw the same man.

"I think whatever is happening, I have a feeling this man knows how to stop it."

My head was reeling as I thought of the man and where I knew him from. "I know who you're talking about. I've seen him, too, in my dreams."

Christina sounded shocked. "What?"

I rubbed my forehead. "I'm headed home."

"But what about the curse?"

"There is something in my closet I need to look through. I think I know where I recognize that man we've been seeing." After I hung up, I packed up the few things I brought up and left out the door, locking it behind me. My feet crunched on the gravel as I made my way to my truck.

Once inside my vehicle, my mind kept thinking of Monica, our research we had done together while she was alive, and the house. Closing my eyes, I tried to remember how the man from the dreams tied into everything. Turning the engine, I sped off down the mountain.

Once I arrived back at the apartment, Christina was seated on the couch. She immediately hopped to her feet when she saw me. There was a moment of silence before I raced over to hold her close to me. I took in the sweet scent of her, and my face buried into her hair. Touching the back of her head, I pulled her closer to me.

"Teddy," she said softly. We stood there holding one another.

After I let her go, I said, "I think I figured out who that man is, but I have to be sure."

Christina furrowed her brow. I headed towards our bedroom. Inside our closet, I kept a box of mementos from the house. Truthfully, it was hard to fully let go of it because my mother was tied to the memory of it, as was Monica. I couldn't just throw them out. Inside the box were pictures we had of Dr. Ransteen, his employees, patients, and family. I found one of the family portraits. It was a black-and-white photo of a lineup of Dr. Ransteen, his brother, his brother's wife, and nephew. My eyes stopped on the nephew.

It was him.

The man from the dreams.

Dr. Ransteen's nephew.

"What is it?" asked Christina from behind me.

I showed her the photo, and she gasped before peering up at me.

"His name was Thomas. He's the nephew of Dr. Ransteen."

"Oh my gosh," she said. "Is he still alive, you think?"

I shrugged. "I have no idea, but he has to know something."

The following day, I contacted Jacob to see if he could find anyone who could track down Thomas. Christina also posted the photo online in the hopes someone might reach out. "I worded it as though we found it somewhere and want to give it back to the family," she said. "Hopefully, someone comes through."

It didn't take long before Christina received a private message on social media. Christina nearly jumped out of her seat at the kitchen table. "I got someone! I got someone!"

I raced over to her.

Christina read the message aloud. "Hi, my name is Becky Sherman. I am a live-in nurse for an elderly man in Chicago. I believe that is him in the photo with his uncle, father, and mother. He told me to give you his number and if you would be so kind as to contact him as soon as possible.

He seems quite surprised and a little shocked by this discovery. Thank you in advance!"

Staring at the telephone number made my heart leap. My palms were sweating.

"Did you want me to call?" asked Christina.

I shook my head. "No, I have to do it." Slowly, I grabbed my cell phone out of my pocket and dialed the number. With each ring, my heart leapt. "H-hello?" I said after the phone clicked. "May I speak with Mr. Ransteen?"

"You are the person with the photo," said a dry and weak voice.

"Yes," I said. I tilted my head. "How did you know?"

"Because nobody has called me Mr. Ransteen in several decades. I changed it to Thomas Richards."

I swallowed. So this was him. "I'm sorry, Mr. Richards."

It was silent. I had no idea what to say. For some reason, my words were stuck in my throat.

The voice over the phone wheezed, "Tell me more about why you have this photo. How long did you live in my uncle's house?"

I blinked as I thought. How did he know all this already? "I... Perhaps a year at the most."

"That's too long," he said.

"What do you mean?" I asked, confused.

"The curse has you."

My stomach churned. "You know about the curse?"

"Of course I know about it," he spat. "And you don't have much time until it takes you completely."

"How did you know I lived in the house?" I asked.

"What's your name?" he asked.

"Ted."

"Ted, nobody would have that photo unless they lived in that home or had ties to it in some way."

He fell silent.

"They can hear us through the walls," he whispered. He was quiet. "They're in your home most likely right now. It isn't safe to talk over the phone."

I swallowed. "What do you mean?"

"But I know how to stop it."

My heart nearly leapt out of my chest. Hope boiled in my chest. "How? What can we do?"

"I've just been waiting for someone to help me," he wheezed again. "We don't have much time. Right now, you can fight back, but not for long. It'll inevitably take over and consume everything in your life."

I hadn't noticed how much my body was shaking. "W-what do I do?"

"You need to get here. I know you don't know me and may not trust me, but I am old. I am dying, so there isn't much I can do to you. This curse… It finds a host it likes and sticks to them like a leech. Have you seen the Beast yet?"

My lips quivered. "N-no. You mean the Beast of Eternal Life?"

"Yes. It's good you haven't seen it yet. That means there's still time, but get here now before it's too late. I'll have my nurse give you all the info you need." Then he hung up.

I gripped the phone in my hand as my whole body shook. If this man was telling the truth, I had to leave fast.

Christina stared at me wide-eyed. "What's going on, Teddy?"

"I know this sounds crazy," I said, "but we have to go to Chicago to meet this man."

"We hardly know him," she said. "Are you sure that's the best idea?"

"We're at a dead end, and he said he knows how to stop the curse."

Christina chewed on her lip. "What if he tries something?"

"He's our best shot."

Christina swallowed. "This all sounds so crazy."

I let out a dry laugh. "All of this does, Christina. Nothing makes sense anymore. I don't even know what reality even is anymore." A migraine stabbed at my head, and I winced. "At this point, I just have to go along for the ride because I'm done fighting it. I'm done trying to make sense of things." I sighed heavily. "What we think is real and not real is not defined…" I thought of what Lavinia said about the astral realm. "We don't know what we don't even *know*!"

Christina's brow pinched in confusion. "What do you mean?"

I shook my head. "Nothing." I fought in my head whether or not to to actually go to Chicago. Christina had a point. Could we really trust a stranger? A stranger related to Dr. Ransteen? Suddenly, my migraine eased. A sense of immediate relief made me close my eyes. I heard Lavinia's voice echo in my head. "Go," she whispered.

Opening my eyes, I stared at Christina, who stood there, picking at her long sleeves. Her eyes were frantic with anxiety.

"We'll leave to Chicago as soon as possible."

Chapter Eight

Chicago

Strapping myself to the seat, I sighed as I stared ahead at the back of the seat in front of me. Christina reached her hand over and grabbed onto mine. She squeezed lovingly, to which I grimaced. I had never flown before, and I wasn't exactly excited about it, considering I wasn't sure if I'd be in control for much longer. However, Chicago would be a long drive, and we didn't want to request more time off from work than we already had.

"You okay, hon?" asked Christina.

I let out a breath and nodded.

"Nervous flyer?" she asked.

I managed a smile and lied, "Yeah."

The flight attendant stood at the front of the plane and took out the phone connected to the wall to speak over the intercom. "Welcome, and thank you for choosing to fly with us today." The flight attendant went on about the safety measures. After that, the plane slowly started to make its way to the runway.

Christina gripped onto my hand and whispered, "It'll be okay. I've flown plenty of times."

I grimaced. The flight wasn't what I was nervous about, but I didn't want to worry Christina any more than I already had. Once the plane took off, I became a little less anxious. It'd be a relatively short flight. I could manage to stay in control of myself for however long it took to get there. We had a couple of hours to kill, so I attempted to sleep. Considering how sleep deprived I was, it was relatively easy despite the turbulence.

A jolt from turbulence startled me awake, however. I gripped onto the handles as I shot my eyes open and peered around. The lights were off inside the cabin, and everyone else seemed to be asleep. Christina's head was slumped over with her eyes closed. I gently moved her head back against the wall of the cabin.

I furrowed my brow. It seemed odd to me that literally *everyone* in the cabin was asleep. The plane shook again, and the lights flickered. Were we going down? My blood ran cold as the thought of crashing raced through my head.

I peered down the aisle in search of a flight attendant, and in the middle of the aisle stood a tall, black, shapeless creature. The air froze, and I rubbed my hands together. The figure didn't move, and nobody else seemed to notice it. Was I hallucinating? A black mist bled out from its sides and slowly consumed the air in the cabin like spider webs.

I fumbled with my belt to unbuckle it so I could escape. The black fog snaked its way closer to me. It wrapped itself around my wrists and forced me to the seat. The figure got more prominent as it floated towards me. My eyes widened, and my heart felt as though it might rip out of my chest. Red, piercing eyes appeared at its head and quickly vanished.

I wanted to scream, but the black tentacles gripped tightly to my neck and squeezed the air out of me. I couldn't breathe. I felt my head swelling as the oxygen was cut off. The figure was now directly in front of me, blocking out everything behind it. It lowered its head towards me, and the red eyes appeared again. The black veins inside it zigzagged menacingly towards its pupil in the center.

"I've got you," I heard a sinister voice say. "You can fight, but I've already dug into your flesh." Pain like a thousand needles poking deep into my nerves shot a fiery pain throughout my body, making me numb. "There is no escaping now."

I managed to shut my eyes and thought of what Lavinia had said. As cheesy as it sounded, I focused on the love I felt for Christina and my mother, sister, and friends. I thought of happy memories—ones that made the warmth grow in my heart. It managed to get rid of the piercing stabs that raked my body, and suddenly I opened my eyes and was sitting in my seat on the plane.

This cheesy stuff worked.

The lights were on, and I peered over at Christina, who was awake reading a magazine. I eyed over the rest of the cabin, and everyone else seemed awake. A flight attendant came around picking up trash from the passengers with a plastic bag. Christina reached her hand out and lovingly laid it on my arm. I turned my attention to her. Her brow was furrowed. "Are you okay?" she asked.

Wiping away the cold sweat from my forehead. I said, "Y-yeah." I let out a breath of relief. It was just a dream. I had to tell myself that because the latter was far too frightening.

Once we landed, we met Jacob and Ben at the gate's exit. Once we'd told them about Thomas, they wanted to tag along. Jacob stood there looking at his watch, holding a briefcase, while Ben was still stuffing his face with the flight's pretzels. We were only visiting for the night and staying at a hotel near the airport. Christina carried her large purse with clothes for tomorrow. She also brought the wooden book along. I swore she could fit the entire world in that damn thing.

"I have someone waiting to pick us up," said Jacob.

Ben cooed. "First class treatment over here."

Jacob chuckled as we walked towards the baggage claim. "I travel a lot to work at different universities, so I know a good chauffeur service."

Once we left the airport, the refreshing Chicago autumn weather embraced me. A man in a suit and hat held up a sign that said, "Williams." Jacob waved his hand, and the driver opened up the door to the black car for us. "Where are we headed?" Jacob asked.

"We're going straight to Thomas's home on the outskirts of the city," said Christina. She handed the address to the driver. "It'll take some time to get there due to traffic, and he wants us to visit him before his midday nap."

Ben, Jacob, and I eyed one another.

"His nurse told me he's in his early nineties," said Christina.

I widened my eyes thinking of my patients back home at the nursing home. "Is he well enough for us to visit him?"

148

"Yes. He seemed to *really* want us to come."

The boys and I looked at one another, and I could tell we had the same thoughts. That could either be a good thing or a bad thing. We took the highway across the heart of the city. It was odd coming to visit Chicago under such strange circumstances. Any other time I would have enjoyed coming to see the sights here and spending the day with Christina at nice restaurants. Instead, we were on a stressful mission to save me from some sort of haunting.

The expression on my face must've been grave because Christina kissed my cheek. "It'll be alright, Teddy."

I managed a smile, but a big part of me didn't believe her. This seemed so far out of our reach. As I stared out the window, I thought of a plan—a way to escape this reality and protect those around me. A lump formed in my throat with the realization of what I may have to do in the end.

We got off the expressway and made our way down a quiet residential area. The trees' branches were bare, and orange and brown leaves colored the ground beneath them. There was something warm about the air in Chicago. The homes all seemed quaint and inviting.

The car stopped in front of a two-story home with yellow paneling. There was a short, cemented walkway that led up to the front door. There wasn't much of a front porch, but there was a smoothed, cemented ramp that led to it rather than steps. The driver opened the door for us, and we stepped out. A bare tree greeted us next to the walkway that led up to the front door. Before we could knock, a middle-aged woman opened the door. She wore a yellow apron over her scrubs.

Her smile reached her eyes. "You must be Thomas' visitors."

Ben waved his hand excitedly. "Hi," he said with a cheeky grin.

"Yes, ma'am," said Jacob as he reached a hand out to shake hers.

"I'm his caretaker, Becky. He's just about finished lunch, so he should have plenty of energy to talk."

She opened the door wider for us to enter. Christina nodded and smiled at Becky, and I shook her hand as I walked past. A staircase led up to the second floor to our right. There was an archway on both sides of the entryway that led into the living room and a dining area. Towards the back was a door that led to what I assumed was the backyard.

"Thomas has been looking forward to your visit," she said. "You can hang your coats on the hook here by the door."

The home smelled fresh of boiled vegetables and chicken. Black-and-white pictures lined the wall on our way to the living room area, including a family portrait. A man stood behind a woman who sat in a chair. Two young children stood on either side of her. The photo had to be from the early 1900s at the earliest. Beside that photo was another colorless one of a young man with his new bride on their wedding day, which looked a lot like Thomas. The last photo was in color, and it was of Thomas as a middle-aged man standing in suspenders and holding an ax, posing with one foot on a log.

I turned my attention to the living room. A small fire was going, and a shriveled man sat in a chair with a blanket over his legs. He was slumped over with his varicose veined and liver-spotted arms resting on the arms of the chair. His wispy white hair was combed back. More age spots could be seen on his head underneath his thin hair.

"Mr. Richards, your guests have arrived," said Becky loudly. She spoke to us in a normal tone, "He is hard of hearing."

Mr. Richards turned his head towards us, and my heart stopped when I saw his eyes. They were the same eyes as Dr. Ransteen's. I swallowed hard. We all took turns shaking his shaking hand.

"I'm Christina," she greeted.

His smile was welcoming and warm. He patted his hand on top of hers slowly. "Yes. You are quite a beautiful young lady."

Christina's cheeks grew pink, which made me smile.

I reached my hand out next, and Thomas's smile vanished when we touched. He stared into my eyes, and I ground my teeth in worry. "You must be Ted," he said.

I managed a nod and swallowed. "Y-yeah. How did you know?"

He looked away for a second as if far off in memory. "I can never forget eyes like that."

I furrowed my brow and looked over at Christina. She shrugged. Jacob reached his hand out to introduce himself along with Ben.

"Ben and I just wanted to help our friends here. It has led us down quite a strange path," said Jacob.

"It did for my uncle too," said Thomas. The mention of Dr. Ransteen made the room heavy. Thomas's eyes wandered around the room. "His spirit is here. Can you feel it?"

Goosebumps crept up my arms and down my spine, and my breathing slowed. "Yes."

Thomas looked me straight in the eye. "Of course you can. His spirit is inside you."

My heart dropped. What did he mean by that?

Thomas was silent for a moment as he looked down at his hands that sat folded on his lap. "I was always embarrassed and grief-stricken over my uncle's past. I wanted to put as much distance between him and me as possible, which was why I changed my last name." His eyes met mine again. "But no matter how hard I try, he always manages to claw his way back into my life." Thomas shrugged. "Perhaps I am cursed." His breathing wheezed. Becky came racing in and hooked him up to an oxygen tank.

"Give him a moment," she said. "I'll get you some tea while he catches his breath." She left towards the kitchen on the other side of the house.

The nursing assistant in me wanted to help, but I knew Becky had it under control. We took our seats on the couch in front of Thomas. The seats were antiques and reminded me of something you'd find in an old Victorian home. The cushions were hardened, and the backrest was uncomfortable. I wiggled a bit as I sat down, trying to get situated. The room was silent except for the sound of the crackling fire followed by Thomas's breathing through the oxygen mask.

Becky came in a few minutes later with a tray full of teacups and a teapot. She poured us each a cup. Christina grabbed the creamer and poured it into her tea. I dropped in one spoonful of sugar and stirred. "Thank you, hon," said Christina.

"Is there anything I can get for you?" Becky asked.

Thomas took off his mask and said, "Yes. Grab that box I had you pull out of the basement the other day." Becky's smile faded immediately, and her jaw muscles tensed. She nodded before leaving towards the staircase.

Becky came in, pushing a large cardboard box across the wood. Jacob, Ben, and I immediately stood up to help carry it the rest of the way towards the coffee table. We took a seat back on the couch.

"How much do you know about my uncle and his story?" asked Thomas. He looked only at me.

I took a big breath in and out as I revisited the night he had me and my mother trapped in my basement. "He owned a mental hospital that ran outside of a large home he owned."

Thomas nodded his head slowly.

I took that as a sign to keep going. "And when his mother got sicker mentally, he wanted desperately to find a cure for her." I paused and spoke more slowly. "He wanted it so badly he started to conduct illegal operations on his patients to find a cure."

Thomas closed his eyes and almost laughed. "Who told you that?"

I wasn't sure if I should answer or not. I looked at Jacob, Ben, and Christina to gauge whether or not I should say anything. "Uh…" I fell silent and chewed on the inside of my cheek. "Your uncle told me."

Thomas opened his eyes. He stared at me point blank and said, "He was lying to you."

153

I didn't know what to say to that, so I fell silent. My muscles were tense with nervousness. I didn't realize I had been grinding my teeth until my jaw started to ache.

"My uncle…" he trailed off for a second. "He was very sick, like his mother, but with an entirely different illness. It started with sleepwalking, the nightmares, and the rage. It got worse to the point he wasn't him anymore. When he started that hospital, he wasn't him anymore. He was…" Thomas shook his head, "something else. You see, my uncle was a kind man. He was a good man who followed an ethical code, but something about my grandmother getting sick made him take a turn for the worse." Thomas put the oxygen mask back on to breathe for a few minutes. "Dr. Ransteen killed his mother that night when she supposedly fell off the roof. She knew her son was no longer her son, and she was trying to escape him when he shot at her. She fell off the roof and died. That is the irony of the entire thing, because he'd started studying medicine to help her."

Again, the similarities between Dr. Ransteen and I sliced through me like a sharp, icy cold knife. I had bought that house for my mother to care for her and hopefully help her through her Alzheimer's. In a way, I sympathized with Dr. Ransteen because he only wanted to help his mother, but he lost himself along the way through the grief. Thomas also reminded me of Lavinia's story and how her boyfriend, who was possessed, had killed her. The realization hit me like a train, and my eyes widened as I thought maybe Dr. Ransteen had been possessed as well.

"My uncle would do anything to help his mother. *Anything*." The room's energy seemed to become even heavier and made the snake in my spine quiver. "I didn't know it at the time, since I was a young boy, but after his death and my family was shamed, I wanted to look for answers. I was hoping to clear my family name, but what I found was much worse. My uncle got himself in a satanic cult of some sort. It's ancient; he got involved in it through H.H. Holmes." Thomas motioned to the box, and Christina and I opened it. Inside were scraps of yellowed paper and thin, leather-bound books that appeared to be falling out of their binding. They were similar to Dr. Ransteen's items we'd found in the basement. At the bottom was a book with thick pieces of paper and a wooden cover. All four of us froze. "I came across these in my search. It's okay. You can touch them," said Thomas.

We picked up the books as if they were a live grenade and handed some of the papers to Jacob to inspect. Jacob's eyes lit up in what I could only assume was excitement as his eyes dug through the articles and books. "Fascinating," he whispered.

Christina dug through her purse and pulled out an identical wooden book. "We have this."

Thomas leaned forward suddenly. "Where did you get that?" His eyes were wide.

"A friend," she said.

"She's dead," added Ben in a sour tone.

"That's probably why she's dead." He motioned to the wooden-covered book. "Few people know about this sort of religion. It is like an exclusive club you only hear from through other members, and those members are scarce."

"What's its name?" asked Jacob.

"This occult or religion or whichever does not have a name. It just *is*."

My body started to hum for some strange reason. It was a peculiar sensation, and I tried to ignore it.

"It started thousands upon thousands of years ago. It can be traced back to Nero." Thomas put the oxygen mask back on to breathe. The name Nero sounded familiar, but I couldn't place it.

Christina gasped.

"You know who that is?" I asked.

Christina nodded. "He was the fifth Roman emperor, and he was a tyrannical ruler. He did terrible things. He even killed his mother by stabbing her to death. He was often associated with working with the devil and being one of the antichrists."

"*One* of the antichrists? You mean there can be more than one?" asked Ben.

"They come and go throughout history," said Thomas. "Before Christ existed, they were called witches or devils. Throughout history, people have come up under this occult's spell and have done horrendous things to mankind."

My forehead creased in confusion.

Jacob found a clear case at the bottom of the box. He lifted it, and he said, "What is in here?"

"It is vacuum-sealed. I found someone who could preserve the stone tablet. It was from Nero's time."

Jacob's eyes widened. "What!?"

Christina, Ben, and I leaned over to eye the gray slab. It had strange symbols engraved on it, much like the symbols I had seen in my visions and Dr. Ransteen's journals along with Monica's book.

"This needs to be in a museum," said Jacob, gripping tightly to the plastic sealed case.

Thomas shook his head. "Then whatever *it* is will be known more widely to the public. My goal has been to stifle it as much as I could."

I swallowed hard, almost not wanting to know the answer. "What is *it*?"

"It's darkness in its purest form. It's the absence of love and happiness. It's the Beast of Eternal Life. It's Abaddon. It's whatever demon name that is out there. It is the devil. It is Satan. It is Nero. It is Hitler. It is Ted Bundy. It is whatever face or name you put to pure evil. It is darkness. It embodies all of that and more. It is the absence of light. It is what makes up hate, anger, and evil."

I shook my head. "I still don't get it."

"It's abstract. Not concrete," said Thomas through wheezing breaths. "It took me a while too because it isn't something you can touch. It is energy. This energy can condense itself and place itself within any one of us to make some of us commit atrocities."

"So it is something without consciousness," said Jacob slowly as if he were trying to understand himself.

Thomas smacked his lips. "I have been trying to figure out if this energy is intelligent or not. Maybe it is something from another dimension we have yet to understand, and I only think it is energy because I cannot see its form. Maybe it has no form. I don't know, but I do know some of our past atrocities have had a connection to these symbols and whatever had its grip on my uncle."

My heart was heavy, and it dropped down to the lowest pit of my stomach. My mouth became dry. There was no hope for me. I frowned as I thought of what I had to do to end this.

"What does this dark energy want? Why does it keep coming back in the form of humans to cause chaos?" asked Christina. She gripped onto my hand, which brought some life back into me.

Thomas paused as he breathed into the oxygen mask. "I think it is something beyond our understanding as mere humans. I think it is much bigger than us."

Jacob rolled his eyes and nearly laughed. "You mean the fight between good and evil?"

Thomas eyed him for a moment. "It has many names, and that is one of them. I call it the fight for balance. There will always be light and dark. You cannot have one without the other, but they seem to always be in competition with one another for dominance. Some people just simply play into the darkness while some play into the light."

That sparked my memory of what Dr. Ransteen had said about how you couldn't have the light without the dark, and he was doing what was necessary. "Your uncle told me something about that."

Thomas nodded. "I bet he did. He was obsessed with that concept, and I didn't understand until I researched further. There is a lot humanity doesn't understand because our science only goes so far. I think if we cannot see it or touch it, then we think it isn't real. That limits us and keeps us from expanding to more advanced science. I believe energy is all around us. It makes up everything. It is what you and I are. It is what my chair is. It is what the ground is, and I believe it is intelligent." He reached his arm out, and it shook as he pointed to the book that sat on Jacob's lap. Jacob gently reached over to place it on Thomas's lap. "This belonged to my uncle. He found it after he spent a summer in

Italy. After that trip, he had changed, and I believe from that point on, he wasn't my uncle anymore. At least not fully. That dark force had taken over him." Thomas unclasped the lock that was bound to the book, and it fell open to reveal a dagger inside of it with Latin words printed on the aged papers. Thomas picked up the dagger. It had a stone handle with a metal blade. Its shine was dimmed with age, and it needed to be sharpened.

"Cool," blurted out Ben.

"This is some kind of ritual dagger," said Thomas. "That much I could gather. I have tried to destroy it, but you cannot." Thomas's hands shook as he held the dagger up. "There is a ritual you do to give yourself to the dark energy, and it'll work through you. As part of the ritual, you must have your blood touch the blade. Once it does, you are part of *it*. All that you are is part of *it*."

I thought of the vision I got of Dr. Ransteen. "Back when I lived in your uncle's home, I had dreams of him in the basement. He had slit his hand within a circle calling for the help of the Beast of Eternal Life."

"Yes, but the Beast of Eternal Life is the same dark energy."

"What can stop it?" asked Christina. Her eyes were blinking like they did when she was trying to think of a solution. "Prayer to God?"

Thomas put the dagger down and closed his eyes, almost annoyed. "This is not about God or the Devil. Those concepts are just representations of *it*. We are all from *it*, and it has two sides: the light and the dark. There can be no life without both of them. You can call it God, Satan, energy, or a spaghetti monster. I call it Source because it is the core of all things."

"So this Source is attacking... itself?" I shook my head and ran my fingers through my hair, thoroughly confused.

"It would seem so, yes," answered Thomas. "Why, I have no idea. It is beyond our comprehension. We think of things as black or white. We think of good and evil as two separate things, but what if it is the same? And we pick and choose which one we will act on, and by so, feeding into whichever side of Source we choose."

My head ached, and I rested my head in my hands as I tried to soak all this in. I didn't know if I quite understood it, but what Thomas talked about was essentially something much bigger than God itself. It was God's God or something to that effect. It was what made up God and all that was good and evil.

After a moment of silence as we sat on this new revelation, Jacob asked, "May I see the dagger?"

Thomas's shaking hand reached out, holding the knife. Jacob was seated further away from him at the other end of the couch, so I reached over to grab the dagger and pass it over to Jacob. However, when my fingers grazed the blade, a sharp shiver raced up my arms and down my spine. It made my brain freeze, and my vision glazed over before blackness inched over my sight.

The blackness was replaced by visions of a young man in a white robe with a blue cloth that hung over his shoulder. His curly, light hair bounced as he stomped across a marble ground with the dagger in his hand. He spoke in a language I couldn't understand as he commanded soldiers.

He passed by giant, marble pillars that cloth hung down from. I noticed he wore brown sandals with straps that wrapped around his ankle.

He entered a room, and a middle-aged woman was sitting in a long chair. She had beautiful, long hair with gold ropes tied around it holding half of it up in a bun. Her long, blue gown fell past her ankles as she stood up in alert. Her face was ashen. She was speaking frantically in a strange, ancient language. It sounded as though she were begging him. The man lunged at her and pinned her to the ground. With the same dagger Thomas had, he stabbed her multiple times. Blood splashed across the walls and curtains of the room. Red liquid oozed out of her mouth as her life slowly left her eyes.

The scenery melted away like wax dripping from a candle, and the image changed to a middle-aged man with a thick mustache and rounded top hat. He appeared to be a proper gentleman until he lured women into alleys before taking them into darkness. Blood oozed out from beyond the closed door once he had them in his clutches.

Finally, everything changed to Dr. Ransteen with the same dagger as he slit his wrists in the basement. He winced from the pain momentarily before speaking in Latin, spreading his blood across a circle that was drawn on the ground.

I heard Thomas's voice chanting in a monotoned voice; it sounded forceful and powerful. The vision began to crumble, and my body vibrated violently. In a snap, I was back on the couch in Thomas's living room. Immediately, I looked at Christina. Her eyes were wide, her mouth open, and her face pale. Jacob's mouth hung open.

"Woah," said Ben. "That's wild."

Thomas held onto one of the soft leather-bound books that laid open.

Immediately, I took my hand off the dagger, and it fell onto the rug. I eyed Thomas who seemed to be the only calm one. "What happened?" I asked frantically.

"He…" Jacob paused. He pointed at the book in Thomas's hands. "Thomas read this verse from the book to bring you back. Your body started convulsing, and your eyes rolled to the back of your head."

"We thought you were having a seizure," Christina said in a panic.

"It worked," Jacob said in awe.

"The book holds counteractive spells, which I think will be beneficial to finding a solution," said Thomas. "That was why I wanted you to come here. I didn't want to risk mailing these items."

We all nodded in understanding.

"I could be wrong," said Thomas, "but I believe this is how you may be able to end the curse, and you can free my uncle." Thomas's lips fit into a tight line before quivering a bit. "Did you see him when you touched the blade?"

I nodded slowly.

Thomas looked down momentarily. "I believe his soul is trapped in the darkness, and only by defeating that energy and rebalancing it can he be freed."

"So what do we do?" asked Ben. "We just read the spells in this book, and then poof! Bye-bye bad man?"

Thomas smiled and chuckled. "If only it were that easy. First, you have to learn how to properly pronounce all

162

the words in the spell or else it won't work. Also, you have to go where the house is. A portal has been opened there, and you have to destroy it."

What Lavinia had told me bounced back to the front of my brain. *The curse had created a portal. The curse that has formed stays in whatever location where the portal has been opened. You must change the portal.* We had to change its energy with the use of the spells.

We had a game plan, but my body nearly shook from fear at the thought we may fail. Christina gripped tightly to my hand. Before we left, Thomas went over the pronunciations of each curse. Jacob wrote in parenthesis the correct pronunciation of this dead language beneath each word in the wooden books. After practicing for a bit, Thomas grew tired, and we left. We were fighting against something much stronger and much more ancient and unintelligible than Satan or some kind of devil. I wasn't sure if we'd be strong enough to stop it.

Chapter Nine
The Portal

W e raced out of Thomas's home, wanting to get back to the house in Saratoga Springs, but our flight wasn't until the following morning. The anticipation of curing my life of this curse was enough to stifle my appetite. We ate at a restaurant next door to the hotel, but I sat in our booth, staring at my glass of water. In my head, I recited over and over the plan to destroy this curse once and for all. This way, it couldn't harm anyone anymore. We'd fly back and immediately go to the house with the wooden book and the other things Thomas had given us.

I thought back to what Lavinia had said. You can't destroy energy because energy never dies, but you *can* change its direction. Perhaps we could change the force of the curse's energy to be light rather than dark. Maybe that was how we stopped it.

Christina reached her hand out to touch my arm. Her brow furrowed. "Aren't ya hungry, Teddy?" she asked.

I let out a slow breath and shook my head. "There's just a lot going on. I can't even begin to think about eating right now."

Christiana frowned a little. "I understand, but ya should at least try somethin'. You're gonna need ya strength for tomorrow." Christina was right, so I looked over the menu again and decided on getting a soup.

That night in our hotel room, I tossed and turned, unable to fall asleep. My heart was beating rapidly from the anticipation. Part of me was fearful I'd get another one of those nightmares where I'd sleepwalk. What if I never came back after that? Nero and the others must know by now what we are trying to do, and what if they fought back? Staying awake was the only way to guarantee I wouldn't lose control.

I stared up at the ceiling, going over the plan in my head. It made the muscles in my chest loosen their grip so I could relax some. The small release of anxiety finally made me realize how heavy my eyelids were. Still, whenever I closed them, my adrenaline hyped up at the thought of falling asleep. My fight with my anxiety was futile, and eventually, I passed out from exhaustion just as the sun was beginning to rise.

My body felt heavy as I slept, which I found strange considering I was asleep. How could one feel their body as they slept? That was when I realized I was dreaming. My body felt heavy as I stayed in this black space of nothingness. I wanted to get up to move, but I felt a dense tug that kept me in place. Lavinia's voice echoed, "Stop. Don't move. They are trying to find you."

I swallowed hard as my blood ran cold.

"Relax," her voice murmured.

Hearing Lavinia was enough to comfort me. I had no idea I had been holding my breath until I could relax enough to allow myself to breathe.

"They are having a hard time finding you," she said.

"Why?" I asked.

Lavinia hushed me gently. "I am cloaking you. They planned to get you tonight to stop you. Sleep or no sleep."

A million thoughts raced through my head, like why they wanted me so badly. Was it to put a permanent end to me? Was it to possess me? Lastly, who exactly were "they"? Nero and Dr. Ransteen only? Or was there more than that? My chest muscles tightened at the uncertainty.

"It'll be okay," Lavinia said. "I'll be with you every step of the way. You are strong."

I doubted that because my fear was far too powerful.

It was as if Lavinia could read my mind. "Fear is not the absence of courage. To be fearful is to be brave. Only fools are arrogant." Lavinia stayed with me as my body got its rest, and knowing she'd be there gave me the comfort to bring back my nerve to stand up to this curse and any non-physical being involved with it.

Christina gently shook me awake. "Teddy, hon."

I stirred and opened my eyes. Christina's smile greeted me, and she bent over to kiss me on the cheek, which softened my heart. "Morning," I said.

"The complimentary breakfast is still available right now. Do you want me to grab you somethin' real quick before we head to the airport?"

Rolling onto my side, I faced her. I thought about my nerves and the flight ahead. "No, I don't think I'm in the mood to eat. Maybe when we land we can go eat."

Christina's grimace told me she wanted me to eat, but she understood my nerves were far too shot to consume anything. "'Kay," she said.

Jacob and Ben met us in the hotel lobby. He checked his wristwatch as he said, "We have a couple of hours before our flight, which should be enough time to get through the check-in progress and all that mess." As we waited for our cab outside, Ben asked, "So what's the plan?"

"We do what Thomas said. We need to go to that house to destroy the portal," I said. I looked at everyone to gauge what they were thinking from their facial expressions.

Christina blinked several times and then nodded. "Okay."

Jacob pressed his lips together and then clicked his tongue. "In that case, I think we should wait for nightfall to go to the house. We don't want anyone to see us."

I agreed with him. When I heard about the sinkhole that had formed after the demolishment, I didn't think much of it. Now I wondered if that sinkhole was actually a representation of the portal.

The flight was thankfully uneventful, and we landed by the afternoon in New York City. Jacob had driven us to the airport, and his car was parked there waiting for us. It was roughly a three-hour drive to Saratoga Springs, and by the time we got there, it was late afternoon. Since it was now the beginning of winter, the sun would be setting in just a couple of hours.

We waited for the long night ahead of us at a diner that was nearby the house. It was a typical greasy spoon that served breakfast, burgers, and fried steak. By that point, I was starving since I hadn't eaten all day. Despite the nerves that were beginning to bubble to the surface, I stuffed down my double bacon avocado burger without a problem.

Christina sat slumped over with her head resting in her hand as she poked at her salad, rolling a grape tomato around on her plate. Jacob sat there, drinking a cup of tea as he stared out the window. Ben was nervous and eating mozzarella sticks. They must all be feeling it at this point. The air at our table was thick with anxious anticipation. I let out a sigh to release some of the built-up tension within me. "I think once we have a detailed plan, we'll be a little less nervous," I said.

"What are ya thinkin'?" asked Christina.

I looked at Jacob and said, "I think we *all* should speak the protection spells. There is strength in numbers, and if we are all part of it, maybe it'll make the spell stronger."

"What if somethin' happens to you in the process?" Christina's voice quivered in fear.

"You mean if I get possessed? I'll be okay," I said with an act of newfound courage I didn't know I had. I thought of Lavinia, and that comforted me. "I have help."

Jacob checked his watch and said, "It's time."

We paid our bill and left for Jacob's car. The first handful of stars shined brightly alongside the quarter moon as we approached the empty property. Soft dirt covered the land where the house once stood. Somehow, the property seemed more menacing now that the home was gone. Perhaps because I knew what really stood there and no demolishment could eliminate the energy that consumed the place.

Jacob gently pulled on the chain-link fence that had been carelessly placed around the perimeter of the plot. It

169

was as if the construction workers didn't care if someone got in or out. We stepped onto the land. My shoes sunk deep into the soft dirt. I held on to Christina's hand and kept her slightly behind me as I walked ahead and stepped slowly as I gauged the danger of our progression. At the center of the property was a large, gaping sinkhole. As I inched closer, some dirt broke off from the edge and fell to the bottom. The sinkhole didn't seem like much in person. It wasn't even that deep, but it was as if the air around it was like a tornado of dense, evil energy. It made goosebumps trickle down my body.

Christina took in a large breath and said, "It's like ya can feel it."

Jacob stood beside me as he stared down at the hole. "I can too."

"I'm feeling it too," said Ben. His stomach growled. "And those mozz sticks."

We were silent as we stared down at the hole. The wind picked up, and I shuddered at the brisk air. I zipped up my jacket and rubbed Christina's arms to warm her up. "Let's get started," I said.

Christina took the wooden book out of her purse. Jacob opened his briefcase and took out the second one. The yellowed pages crinkled as they opened them to the protection spell page. At the bottom of his briefcase, I noticed he had the metal dagger. I picked it up and immediately dropped it in the dirt as the searing pain of fire consumed my hand. I grabbed at my hand and clenched my teeth.

"What's the matter?" Christina asked. She went to pick up the dagger.

I yelled, "Don't! It feels like fire when you touch it." I shook my hand as I tried to rid myself of this affliction, but it felt as if the burning sensation was permanently stuck to my skin. My hand grew hotter by the moment. It became almost unbearable. "Just start!" I yelled at Jacob through gritted teeth.

Jacob fumbled with the book, and he cleared his throat as he read the spell out loud. It was a rough start from them because we had just learned this language, but they followed along with Jacob's written pronunciation guide, and they steadily got better with it. Christina hesitated as she stared at me. Her brow creased in concern. At first, I wasn't sure if any of this would work. We must have looked crazy out there saying this spell, but Thomas's theory was our best bet.

I figured the burning wouldn't go away, so I willed myself to concentrate on speaking the spell rather than focus on my hand. The spell was several pages long, and once we finished through all the pages, we'd start all over again with reciting it.

I thought something physically would happen, but the ground didn't rumble. The dirt didn't move. The air still felt cold and brisk. As we continued to chant the spell, my body slowly began to warm up. I noticed Christina started to take off her jacket, as did Jacob and Ben. Despite it being forty degrees, our bodies were heating up. Steam rose from our bodies. Looking down at my hands, I noticed my body was doing the same thing. On the ground, and the dagger burned bright orange as it sank deeper into the dirt.

We all observed this, but we never stopped reciting the spell. Whatever was going on, it had to be working to some degree. My body lurched in pain as the burning got worse. It felt as though I were on fire. I fell to my knees as sweat drenched my clothes. The burning sensation was like a thousand knives sizzling into my flesh. Christina, Ben, and Jacob stopped chanting as they, too, fell to the floor. "W-we can't stop," I seethed.

Christina screamed out in pain as her muscles tightened and she curled inward. My heart twisted, and I instinctively reached out to her. Jacob let out a yell before he went back to reciting the spell. Ben was panting and yelling out. His body was sprawled out in the dirt. I managed to crawl over to Ben. "Recite the spell," I said through gritted teeth. "Distract yourself."

Ben yelled out again. "Monica!" Suddenly, his body froze, his eyes widened, and he let out one final gasp.

"Ben!" I began shaking him. "Ben!"

"What happened to him?" Christina asked in between painful tears.

"I-I don't know! But we can't stop what we started." The more we chanted, the more our bodies felt like we were on fire. Christina continued to scream. Finally, she spat before getting onto her knees. Her body shook as she continued to chant the spell along with us, and I laced my fingers through hers.

Suddenly, I felt a rush of wind push me back, and my body went rigid. Christina moaned as she made her way over to me. Jacob yelled out, "Don't... stop." Christina paused before going back to quoting the spell.

My vision blackened as I lost control of myself. I could no longer see, and then I felt a cold rush pull me up and out of my body. Floating above the scene, I witnessed my body seizing in the dirt. Foam seeped from my lips. Instinctively, I went to help myself, but Ben's hand stopped me. I looked up at him. "I have to help myself from dying!" I implored him.

"There's nothing you can do for yourself, man."

"Did we die?" I asked frantically.

Ben shrugged. "Beats me."

A familiar, raspy feminine voice spoke up from behind us. "You will not die, but there is nothing you can do at the moment other than to help your friends."

I gazed back down at my body, and my eyes widened as dark shadows swarmed around my body. "What is that?" I yelled.

"The darkness," said the voice. "The curse."

"H-how do I stop this?" I asked. I ran my fingers through my hair and tugged.

"By relaxing and giving strength to your friends," it said. "They're here. Hurry."

Ben's eyes widened as he peered behind my shoulder. "Oh shit!"

Following his gaze, there was a giant cloud of black storming towards us. It enveloped anything and everything in its wake. I didn't know how to help other than to start reciting the spell from my end. Ben and I went closer to Jacob and Christina to help them with reciting the spell. As we did this, I felt the air become cooler. Despite not being in a physical body, I could still feel the wind. There were also new things I could feel, like how Christina was feeling. Her body, and Jacob's, still felt like they were on fire. I could *feel* their fear as if it were a tangible thing like a breeze.

"Emotions are thicker here on this side of things," said the feminine voice. Suddenly, Lavinia appeared before me.

Ben paused with his mouth agape.

"In this dimension, the untouchable becomes touchable. You can help them better in this realm because you can manipulate energy more easily," said Lavinia. "Stay focused, Ben." She smiled pleasantly.

"I-is Monica with you? Is she okay?"

Lavinia nodded. "She is. You will see her soon."

Ben and I recited the spell, and I could feel the burning pain lift gradually from both Jacob and Christina. It was similar to if I were to step out from a furnace into the snow. It was as if we were sharing the same pain, and we all felt its release at once. Christina let out a sigh, and they took a momentary pause as they caught their breath. I said out loud, "Don't stop reciting the spell."

I don't think they heard me, but Jacob said, "I think we should continue despite the pain being gone."

Christina looked over at my body that had now stopped seizing. My muscles were still rigid with my hands curled inward towards my chest. "But Ted… and Ben."

I said, "I will be fine. You must destroy the portal in order to help me."

Christina furrowed her brow. "I have a feeling, though, that the best way to help him is by using the spell."

Jacob nodded his head in agreement, and they both went back to speaking the ancient language.

The stench of sulfur filled the air as the dark cloud finally reached us and shrouded our sight. It was like I was back in the black abyss from my dreams. I became consumed by freezing ice. I yelled out, but the fog of blackness was thick. It was like trying to move through thick mud as I attempted to fight back. "You can't stop us," A sinister voice said. As I continued to flail at the dark, thick masses, a face appeared. I recognized him from the vision I'd had before. It was Nero. His curls wrapped around his face, and his thick eyebrows remained furrowed over his bright eyes. "We are too strong now," he said.

The face morphed and changed to H.H. Holmes. "And there is nothing you can do to stop us."

The face changed yet again to Dr. Ransteen's. "We have been within you too long."

Ben tried to take a swing at the darkness, but it was futile. Fighting in this dimension was different. I didn't think attempting physical blows would work in a non-physical world.

The darkness laughed, which made my body rumble. My astral body's reaction to its laughter reminded me emotions and energy were what ruled this realm. "You have to think of love and happiness to fight it," I told Ben.

"Monica," he whispered to himself, and his body took on a white glow all around it.

I focused on thoughts of Christina, my mother, my sister, and my friends once again. Thinking of every happy memory I'd ever had, I felt myself get stronger, and with that, I noticed the black mass started to evaporate slowly.

I called out for Lavinia, and I could see a bright streak of white light slice through the black mass before appearing beside me. The fog formed again and darted towards Jacob and Christina. I yelled out as I raced over to them. Acting purely on instinct, I jumped into the black mass. Ben followed behind me.

Christina and Jacob couldn't see what was happening, but they were reacting to it because they both began to scream. They grabbed ahold of their ears and began to shake uncontrollably on the ground. "We must give them strength!" yelled Lavinia. "You have to work as a spirit does in this world. Recite the spell, but imagine your energy becoming bigger as you do so. Focus on your love and joy."

That was easier said than done because my fear was much stronger than my joy at the moment. My doubt in myself was dampening how strong I could get my energy to be, and I knew it. It was strange and foreign to me to vividly feel what my thoughts and emotions could do no differently than how you felt a physical sensation in a body. I was new to this realm. I had just learned how energy worked. Just a few years ago, I never thought any of this stuff was real. How could I be strong enough to defeat whatever this was?

"Stop!" Lavinia yelled. Her white energy continued to break through the black mass. "Your thoughts can be felt and heard. It takes form here and becomes you and everything around you. Stop it. Focus." She peered behind her. "The beating heart of the curse is reaching closer. We don't have much time. Once it consumes you, you will all die."

"I got this, bud," said Ben. He inched himself through the black mass where I could no longer see him. I had to fight past the thick mud of fog, and I used my typical bull-headedness to my advantage to make my way through. The air became thick like jelly, and the black abyss became darker, like a matte dark.

"Don't go in there," warned Lavinia.

"I have to help Ben."

"He is in the curse's core, and there is no returning once you go in."

I froze. "H-how can I help him, then? Why would he do that?"

Lavinia smiled. "To save your lives."

Bright, thin strands of white light broke through the darkness's mushy core. It was hair thin but starkly noticeable against the matte black.

"He's stronger than I am," I said.

"His love for Monica is strong," said Lavinia. "Christina needs you."

I raced over to her and placed my hands on their shoulders. Shouting the spell, I mustered up all the courage and strength I had left. My chest expanded and warmed at the thought of Christina's smile, and then flashed to my mother, reading me bedtime stories when I was a child.

Christina and Jacob must've felt my energy because their screaming ceased. They lay curled in a fetal position in the dirt before unraveling themselves slowly. Christina had her teeth gritted in pain as she continued to speak the spell. Jacob was able to continue the fight as well. Lavinia had made her way over to me. "We must get rid of the dagger's power," said Lavinia.

I thought about how we could do that.

Lavinia heard my thoughts and said, "We need someone from the physical to be holding the dagger as we chant the protection spell."

I spoke in Christina's ear. "Go to the dagger. Destroy the dagger." I repeated myself until she eventually acted on my words.

"The dagger, Jacob," she said. "We have to get rid of its power too." She crawled across the dirt and clung to the small weapon. She immediately dropped it and grabbed her hand as she clenched her teeth.

"It's too painful for her," I said.

"The pain isn't actually affecting her physically," Lavinia said. "It just feels like it is in order to protect itself."

I was surprised as I saw Christina grab her jacket and use it as a barrier between her skin and the dagger as she held it. She spoke in the dead language again, and the air vibrated violently. My entire being shook as I heard several voices all speak at once in a panic. It was a mixture of male and female voices, and I peered over to my right and noticed the black cloud that hovered over Jacob was now making its way over to Christina and me. Bracing myself for impact, I used my astral body to shield Christina, if only a little bit. Lavinia appeared behind me. I knew that because I could feel her warmth and smelt that sweet, spicy scent which always surrounded her.

"I'll protect you," Lavinia said.

Going back to repeating the spell alongside Christina, a white stream floated overhead. It was like a smooth liquid encased us three into a protective bubble. Directly above, the black masses surrounded us, and the bubble cracked and broke apart as I felt their dense energy pound at the barrier. It made my body shake and vibrate.

Not wanting to stop, I continued with the spell. I could hear Ben's voice as he chanted, and I was relieved he was still here. The dagger changed from orange to crimson red as it continued to glow even brighter. Christina faced away from it as her eyes squinted. The smell of sulfur seeped through our encasement, and I knew they were managing to break through. The glowing red dagger changed color again, and I tilted my head to one side as I witnessed blue crack through amongst the crimson.

A terrible shriek, like metal scraping against cement, halted the air. Even Christina perked up. I winced from the sound of it. The air shuddered violently and my vision blurred as more cracks of blue broke through the dagger.

The black mass finally managed to break through and shoved me with such force I flew across the plot. It felt like life was pushed out from me, and I came to a halt at the other corner of the property. Immediately, I searched for Christina and saw she had been flung as well, but in the other direction. She rolled over onto her side before pushing herself up to her knees.

Above where the dagger lay, the dark mass stirred around erratically into shapeless forms. I ran over to the dagger and saw it was completely blue. I had no idea what that meant, but it had to be good because as the dark mass spun and jagged about, pieces of white orbs floated out. As they trickled out, it made the mass become smaller. Staring in awe, Lavinia came to my side. Her energy felt weakened. The typical glow around her was now dimmed. "You did it," she said in a low tone. "The curse is destroyed."

"What is happening now?" I asked.

"The souls that were once trapped by the curse can now be freed," she said.

"We destroyed all darkness?" I asked, surprised.

Lavinia's glow came back a little as she laughed. "No. You can never destroy all darkness because then there would be no light. You cannot have one without the other."

The air softened as the thick fog shrunk. It was as if I could breathe again. At its center was Ben, who was now curled into a fetal position. His light was completely gone. "Ben!" I wanted to race over to him, but Lavinia stopped me.

"There is nothing you can do for him now."

"What do you mean?" My brow furrowed.

"He gave all his light to the curse in order to destroy it."

My voice became more panicked. "What does that mean!"

Lavinia peered over at me.

Suddenly, Ben's astral body vanished, and in its wake was a bright white orb. It rocketed over to me. Ben's body took form again, but it wasn't as dense as before. It was simply an outline of him and his characteristics. "Good job, bud. We did it. Now I can go be with Monica." His silhouette vanished, and his orb left up towards the sky before disappearing.

I felt my entire body shake in pain. "W-what will the souls do once they are all freed?" I asked.

"Some will probably not want to be in the light, and they will find something else to latch themselves onto that matches their dark energy. However, some will choose the light since now they have the freedom of choice. The curse prevented them from their own free will. Ben will go to the light where Monica is."

One final orb came out from the abyss, and a silhouette took form to reveal Dr. Ransteen. The same faint, white glow that was around Lavinia was now around Dr. Ransteen. "Thank you," his voice echoed before he evaporated.

I peered over at my body, which now lay limp on the ground.

"It won't be easy once you return to your body. It has been through a lot tonight. Great pain awaits you," said Lavinia.

I let out a sigh. "Is there any way I can zap that pain away?"

Lavinia smiled, almost laughing. "No."

"Damn," I shrugged. I stood above my body. Once I was close enough, it felt like the air was being sucked out of me as everything went black once more.

After a moment of nothingness, I felt heavy, like an anchor was laying on top of me. I slowly opened my eyes and saw Jacob and Christina staring down at me. Jacob was checking my pulse on my arm. "He's alive," he said.

Christina let out a quivering breath as tears stained her cheeks. "Teddy, hon," she said.

Lavinia was right. My muscles screamed in pain, and I could barely move my neck. Christina ran her fingers through my hair and kissed my cheek.

"How are you feeling?" asked Jacob.

Closing my eyes, I focused on my breathing. "Terrible, but alive." I managed a tight smile. "Ben…" I trailed off and looked over where his rigid body lay.

Jacob went over to him and tried to wake him up. He checked his pulse before immediately doing CPR.

Wincing, I sat up on my elbows. "Jacob," I called out in a hoarse voice.

Jacob peered over at me as he continued pressing on Ben's chest.

I shook my head.

Jacob looked down at Ben before slowly stopping. He sat back, with a hand on Ben's chest, and closed his eyes. A painful cry broke out from within Christina. She covered her mouth as the tears fell.

I eyed the sinkhole, thinking of Ben. "I think we were able to do it, bud."

"I do too," I heard his voice say. Wincing, I grabbed ahold of Christina's hand. "You did great."

Christina's tears were thick, and I kissed them away as I held her close to me.

Jacob stood up and called emergency services on his phone. He took his jacket to place over Ben's body before making his way over to me.

I clenched my teeth in pain as Jacob helped me to my feet. Slinging my arms over him and Christina, they helped walk me back to the car. My muscles groaned and my joints popped at every movement, but once I was in the vehicle, I let out a breath of relief. The air around the property felt lighter, and, while I hadn't noticed it before, the strange darkness that surrounded the plot was now gone. You wouldn't have noticed it unless you were paying attention, but the light seemed to shine on the property now. It especially shined eloquently around Ben, who I knew was now with Monica and his father.

I lay my head back against the seat and let the bittersweet feeling of losing my friend to the afterlife take over me. My chest ached, but knowing where he was helped.

Paramedics showed up. They attempted to resuscitate Ben, but it was no use. He had been dead long before they showed up. Christina stood crying as Jacob gave a report to the police about what happened. We said Ben fell into the sinkhole and had a seizure from hitting his head in the fall. It was the only thing we could fathom would make sense to them.

Peering up at the night sky, I let the gentle breeze hit my face. I could breathe again without a heaviness weighing down on me. In each blow of the wind, I could feel Ben, Lavinia, Monica, and my mother. It was as if I was much more sensitive to it now.

Jacob drove me and Christina to the hospital to get my body checked out. The police didn't question my injuries were from falling into the sinkhole. I sat in the hospital and thought of my last visit here three years ago after being held hostage at that house. I couldn't help but find the humor in it. Much like Ben would. That damn house was going to make my medical bills go up.

Christina came into my room with some Jell-O. "I got you a treat," she said with a small smile.

"Oh good," I said. "We'll have to call Ben's mother."

Christina was quiet. "I know."

I reached out and grabbed ahold of her hand. "He's okay."

Christina stared me in the eye and nodded.

Now, my life could go back to normal, but I knew I wouldn't ever be the same. The things I knew now I couldn't ever unknow. All that was left now was to make sure nobody ever got ahold of that book again.

The End